ACKNOWLEDGEMENT

To my wonderful husband, thank you for always supporting me. To my mother, thank you for all your help. To my children, never give up on your dreams.

Forgotten Past

Rebecca Haddock

Prologue

"Chelsey, I'll take that pot of coffee. My 4:00 a.m. friend is back," Aurora said through the window that opened to the kitchen in the back of the cafe. She turned and walked towards the man who had just sat down at the table in the corner. "Good morning," she said to him with a smile. "Good morning," he replied, returning her smile. "I've got the coffee coming, do you want a menu?" she asked him. She always asked him, and he always declined.

The man had been coming into the café at 4:00 a.m. every morning for about the last two weeks. He only ordered coffee, and he always came in alone. Sometimes he would write in a journal he carried, and sometimes he would read a book. He would carry on a conversation some mornings with Aurora if she did not have any other customers. He always left her a big tip.

Aurora walked around the counter and grabbed a coffee cup and the pot of fresh coffee that Chelsey had set in the open window. "Thanks, Chelsey," Aurora told her friend. They had both been working this shift together for a little over a year now. They were rather good at anticipating what the other needed.

Aurora went back around the counter and began wrapping silverware in napkins that they would need later in the day. She glanced at the man every once in a while, wondering again what brought him to the café every morning. He never seemed to be in a hurry to go anywhere, and usually sat at the table long after the coffee was gone.

Aurora had gotten used to this man, although she did not know his name. The first time he came into the café she had noticed he was an attractive man. He was always dressed casually in blue jeans and a t-shirt. The cowboy boots completed the look. He had brown hair that was cut off the ears and shoulders, and he had a very nice smile. He seemed to be just a few years older than she was.

Aurora had not dated much since high school, but she would not mind a date with him. She wondered again what brought him to the café every morning, but she was too hesitant to ask. She did not even know his name. She felt herself blush at her thoughts and turned her attention back to the silverware she was wrapping, hoping the man did not notice.

When she saw the man get up from his table, she walked towards him. "Will we see you tomorrow?" she asked him. She had never asked him this before, but he smiled at her. "It's a possibility," he said. "I'm Aurora, by the way," she told him. "It's very nice to meet you, Aurora," the man said, but he did not introduce himself. He turned and walked out the door and Aurora was left watching his back.

Aurora was left to her thoughts once the man left, and she wondered who he was and why he started showing up every morning. She had a lot of questions, but she would not ask them. She was curious, but she had never been nosey. It was none of her business. So, she got back to work.

She was grateful when the lunch crowd thinned out. Monday mornings might be slow, but lunchtime was crazy. She never got off work on time on a Monday. However, it had been a great day for tips. When she finally walked out of the restaurant at the end of her shift, she sighed in relief that her day was finished and headed to her car.

As she pulled out of the parking lot, she did not see the men watching her from a car parked across the lot. She did not notice that they pulled out of the parking lot behind her. She left the lot and headed for home. The car behind her followed at a steady pace, keeping a good distance between them. They could not afford to get caught tailing her. They had only been told to watch her, and until they were told something else, they would not be seen.

Chapter 1

Aurora

The next morning, I made my way into the cafe. I was dragging. I had not slept well, and I had dreamed some crazy dreams. The dream had started with my parents. I had been too young when they died to remember them, but my grandparents had pictures of them in the house where I had been raised. In my dream, my parents looked just like they did in those pictures. It was not the first time I had had this dream.

My parents and I were at a carnival. It was evening and the lights on the rides were brilliant. I was in awe as I watched all the people moving around me. I could hear laughter and talking coming from all around me, and I could feel my mother's hand in mine, holding on tightly. "Do you want to ride a ride?" I heard her voice from above me and I just nodded, not taking my eyes away from the activity around me.

The tilt-a-whirl was my favorite ride and I knew we were heading that way. We gave the man at the gate our tickets and stepped up the stairs to the platform where the cars sat waiting. When the ride started, the three of us were laughing as the car spun and moved around the platform. I felt my stomach lurch each time the car changed direction and I giggled. But then the dream changed.

Suddenly, the open car we were in was no longer on the platform, and I heard my parents screaming beside me. I was hurled through the air and rolled across the ground. When I stood and turned, I looked at where my parents lay on the ground. They were covered in blood and their eyes were open, but they were not moving.

I saw men approaching. It seemed they were coming from every direction. Their hands were out as if they were going to grab me. They were watching me with intense, menacing looks, and I knew I had to run. I turned away from them and ran, but I knew they were following me. I ran into a dark forest. The tree branches scraped and grabbed at me as I ran. I ran as fast as I could until I felt myself panting from the exertion. There were only trees around me, but I could hear the sounds of the men following me. Their voices reached me, but I could not tell what they were saying or how close they were.

Pushing my way deeper into the trees, I continued to run. Suddenly, I felt myself falling. The ground had given way underneath me, and I fell into what seemed like a bottomless hole. I continued falling for a long time, wondering if I would die when I hit the bottom. No scream left my mouth as I clenched my teeth tightly together so the men following me would not know where I was. When I landed, it was on something soft. There was no pain as I had anticipated, and everything around me was quiet. I could not see where I was as the night had turned to complete blackness.

I heard voices from high above me, and I stayed quiet as I listened to the voices. They were looking for me, but they had not fallen into the hole. Suddenly, a hand clamped over my mouth, and I heard a voice whisper beside my ear. "Don't say a word. You have to hide, or they will find you," the voice said. That was when I sat up in the bed and opened my eyes.

The dream had seemed so real, and I was glad to be awake from it. I had dreamed about my parents before, and the dreams always scared me. I always woke with my heart racing and in a cold sweat. I took a few minutes to try to calm my breathing. It was only a dream and it was not real. I pushed the thoughts of the dream away and got out of bed. I was definitely going to need some coffee this morning.

At 4:00 a.m., the man entered the diner and took his usual seat in the corner. I got a carafe of coffee and a cup and took it to his table. I smiled at him, but I could tell the smile did not reach my eyes. I was a wreck this morning and I probably looked as bad as I felt. I poured him some coffee and asked him if he would like a menu. I already knew he would decline. "No, thank you. Just the coffee for me," he said, and my eyes flew open wide. His was the voice from my dream! The man who had told me to run. Somehow, my overactive imagination was hearing his voice in my head.

I turned quickly from the table, hoping he had not seen my reaction when he spoke. Maybe I just needed more sleep. These early morning hours were killers to begin with, and now, adding a sleepless night, I was doomed. When I took the man his bill, he looked up at me with a kind expression. "Are you doing okay today?" he asked me softly, and I was surprised by his question.

"Yeah, I think I just need more sleep," I told him. "I think I will take a menu today after all," he replied, and I must have given him a funny look because he laughed. "A man's gotta eat," he said. I just smiled at him as I turned and walked away, returning with a menu a few moments later. There was no one else in the café, so I waited at his table for his order.

"Aurora is a beautiful name," he said softly, his eyes never leaving the menu. "Thank you," I replied startled. "I'm David, by the way," he continued. "Nice to meet you, David," I replied, and he turned his head until his eyes met mine. His look was intense, and for a moment I could not look away. I was relieved when he finally gave me his order and I had something to focus on as I wrote his order on my notepad.

"I'll go put this in," I told him, and turned from the table. I was feeling completely shaken, and I needed to get myself under control. Obviously, I was way more exhausted than I thought. Once Chelsey started on his order, I looked back to the table and found David watching me. The intensity from before was gone, but I was still unnerved. I had no idea why. David was very handsome, and his smile made me smile. It must have been the dream that had me unsettled.

When his food was ready, I returned to his table and set the plate down in front of him. "Do you have a few minutes?" he asked me, and I nodded and sat down at the table across from him. "So, tell me something about yourself," he said. I wondered about his sudden interest in talking, and also, his sudden interest in me.

"Well, there's really not much to tell," I said. "My parents died when I was young, my grandparents raised me, and I work here. That's pretty much my whole life," I told him honestly. The intense look was back in his eyes, and I wondered about it as he ate.

"And you?" I asked him, wondering what brought him to the café every morning. "I'm a writer," he told me. "I like to study human behavior and watch how people interact," he continued. "And so, you come to the café to observe me?" I asked him, surprised that I had been so bold in my question but wondering if that was the reason he was here. It was the first thing that had come to mind when he said he liked to watch people.

He was not surprised by my question but smiled over at me instead. "Well, it is kind of hard not to observe the only person in the room with you, don't you think?" he asked me as he continued to eat, a hint of a smile on his lips. I thought about this for a minute. I really hoped he was not observing me for something he was writing.

"I won't be seeing my name in any books, will I?" I asked him and he chuckled. "No, you are safe from that," he replied. There were a few moments of silence as he took another bite, then he looked up at me. "If there is nothing more to your life than what you have just told me, I guess I have to ask what you do for fun?" he surprised me by asking. "Fun. I guess I have grown out of having fun," I told him seriously. This made him laugh, and I felt the smile on my lips.

"You are never too old for fun," he said. It had been a different kind of childhood for me. My grandparents had raised me, but they had lived outside of town. There were no neighbors and no children for me to play with, other than at school. It really had been quite a lonely childhood.

"I didn't mean to turn you so sad," I heard and looked up at David. He had stopped eating and was watching me. "It's okay. I was just thinking about how I had quite a lonely childhood," I told him honestly, not sure why I was revealing so much of myself to him. "I had a dog and some cats, but never really any people around. My grandparents were older when I went to live with them, and they showered me with love and attention, but no other people," I said softly.

"So, where do you see yourself in ten years?" David asked me. "Honestly, I have never thought that far ahead," I told him. "I pretty much take it one day at a time. Life likes to throw me curve balls and I have gotten pretty good at dodging them so far," I continued. David laughed. "It wouldn't be life without a few curves," he said.

I heard the café door open, and the little bell attached alerted me to the new customers. "I've got to get back to work," I said, turning from the door back to David. There was a look in his eyes that scared me for a moment. He was not looking at me, but instead, at the two men that had just entered the café.

I wondered about that look as I stood from the table and planted a smile on my face. Turning, I headed towards the table where the two men were sitting. "Would you guys like some coffee this morning?" I asked. Neither of them spoke, but they both nodded. "I'll be right back with some menus," I told them, and walked back behind the counter.

Chapter 2

I watched the three men in the room. David watched the other two men, but they seemed unaware. I took the coffee to their table and handed them each a menu. I smiled and told them I would be back for their orders, but neither of them smiled or spoke. It made me feel a little creeped out, but I made my way back to David's table with his check.

When I set the check down on the table, David reached for my wrist and held it. His eyes locked with mine and I could not look away. He reached for the pen and I saw him write something on the check. "You are in danger," I read, and I looked back up at him in alarm. I wondered if he knew something about the two men that had just been seated.

He released my wrist, then wrote more. "Go out the back door." My eyes opened in surprise. I wondered if he thought the two men were going to try to rob us. I had not seen any guns, but for some reason, I trusted that David had seen something that I had not. I nodded in silent agreement, then walked away from his table and into the kitchen.

I grabbed Chelsey's hand and pulled her to the back door with my finger over my lips, indicating for her to stay silent. When we stepped out the back door, Chelsey gave me a worried look. "What's wrong?" she asked me. "I'm not sure," I told her. "David seems to think we are in danger from those two men in there," I explained.

I saw the car pulling up and saw David behind the wheel. "Get in," he said, and I indicated the back seat to Chelsey. "No, not both of you. Just you," he told me seriously. I took a step back from the car. I did not know this man, and I definitely was not getting in a car with him by myself. He had only just told me his name today.

"Aurora," he said softly. "You are the one that is in danger. Not her," he said, pointing at Chelsey. "Look, I don't know what this is about, but I have to get back inside. I can't just leave with you," I told him. "Chelsey, can you give us a moment?" David asked. "I'll go see what's going on inside," she said, and walked back in the door of the cafe.

"Aurora, those two men inside have been following you for over a week now," he told me. I felt my jaw drop in disbelief. "But why?" I asked. "I don't have all the answers, but I do know this is the first time they have let you see them and there is a reason for that. I assure you that reason is not good," he said.

Just then the back door opened, and Chelsey walked outside. "Aurora, I don't know what's going on, but those two guys in there are very interested in where you are," she said with a worried look. I glanced up at her in surprise. "Just go," she said softly, pointing at David. I walked around and got in the car. He had some explaining to do.

David put the car in drive and sped out of the parking lot. I glanced back at the café and saw the two men exit the front door. They saw me, and quickly headed to their car. I looked over at David. He had seen the same thing in the rearview mirror. I felt the car pick up speed and I reached for my seatbelt, clicking it around me.

Neither of us spoke as David guided the car through traffic, taking random turns and accelerating to crazy speeds. If I were not so terrified, I might have tried to talk some sense into myself. However, my thoughts were all jumbled as I watched in the side mirror as David tried to lose the car that was following us. We had gotten quite a bit of a head start before they got to their car, but I could still barely see them in the distance.

David had said that I was in danger. Obviously, those two men wanted something from me, but I had no idea what. David had also said that they had been following me. How did he know that? Was he following me too? I was definitely afraid of those men, but I did not know if I should be afraid of David as well.

It was a full half hour later that I felt the car begin to slow and I turned and looked behind us. "I lost them," David said, glancing in the mirror once again. "Who were they?" I asked him, wondering if he even knew. "Hired men," he said. "Hired? Hired for what?" I asked, feeling more questions come to mind, but afraid that David might not have the answers.

"I'm assuming they were hired to get you," he said, and my jaw dropped. "I don't understand. Why would someone hire them to get me? What would someone want from me?" I asked, and I watched David glance over at me. "And how is it that you knew they were watching me? Have you been following me too?" I finally asked, afraid of what his answer might be.

"Look, Aurora, I only have half of the answers about what is going on and I will give them to you. But I am going to warn you now that you are not going to like it," he replied, giving me a look that let me know he was serious. I felt my body shudder and asked the next question that popped in my head. "Am I safe with you?"

I saw David's expression soften as he glanced at me again. "I would never hurt you," he said gently, and I heard the truth in his voice. I turned my eyes back to the road. "Where are we going?" I asked him, noticing we had left my small town. "You aren't safe here anymore. You can't go back," he replied. My eyes opened wide in alarm.

"What do you mean I can't go back? Ever? What about my apartment. My job. Am I just supposed to disappear and pretend my life here doesn't exist? Am I supposed to be on the run for the rest of my life? With you?" I asked anxiously. I felt so helpless right now, and I really hated the feeling.

"I have been hired to keep you safe, and you will be safe with me. And yes, you can never go back," David replied. The feeling of helplessness was quickly replaced by anger. "You were hired to watch me?" I asked, my voice giving away my frustration. "Who hired you?" I asked him next.

"Your father," David replied, and my jaw dropped open in surprise. That was definitely not what I had expected him to say. "My father is dead," I replied adamantly. The look David gave me told me that he had been completely serious. I had no words. I could not think of anything to say as I thought about what he had just told me. I tried to think about my parents.

I had no memory of them. Somehow, I managed to dream about them often, but those dreams were not pleasant ones. I needed answers from David, but I did not know what questions to ask. If my father were really alive, then why was I told that he was dead and my grandparents raised me. If David really had been hired by my father, then that meant my father knew where I was.

I turned and looked out the window. It really did not matter where we were going, so I did not ask. David just kept driving. We were already far away from my hometown of Salina, Kansas. He said he would tell me what he knew, but I was not so anxious to hear it anymore. My grandparents had lied to me. Well, David said my father was alive. I did not know if I could trust him. Sure, he saved me from whoever those men were, but he basically did the same thing those guys were trying to do. He took me away from everything and everyone that I knew.

I did not know what to think, so, I just waited, and David drove. After about an hour, I realized we were heading towards Wichita. I wondered if that was our destination. David had not gotten on the interstate but stayed on back roads. Once we entered the Wichita city limits, it seemed David knew where he was going. We turned down street after street until we reached a residential area. When he finally pulled into a driveway, I looked up at the house in front of us.

David pulled the car into the garage and shut the garage door behind us. Then he turned and looked at me. "Welcome to my home," he said, and opened the door and got out. The questions I wanted to ask started filling my head, but I remained quiet as I got out of the car and followed David to the door that led into the house.

We stepped into a modern kitchen. The house from the outside was a typical ranch-style home, and I was surprised by the modern feel when I walked in. The kitchen had all white cabinets and stainless-steel appliances. The countertops were all black granite and the floors were all a dark, almost black, hard wood.

The kitchen was open to the living room and the same floors continued into that room. I followed David through the kitchen, and he sat down on a white couch. "Come. Sit down," he said to me, and I sat down in a plush white armchair across from him. Hopefully, he was ready to talk.

I watched him for a long quiet moment, and he looked at his hands clenched in his lap. Finally, he looked up at me. "I was not supposed to tell you any of this, but as they have found you, circumstances have changed. You were supposed to live out the rest of your life in peace and be happy. Now I don't know what to do with you," he said, and I heard a worried tone in his voice.

"You don't know what to do with me?" I asked incredulously. "You took me away from my home, my job, my friends, and you tell me that I can't go back. You better figure out what to do with me, and quickly, because now you are stuck with me. How about you start by telling me what in the world is going on. You said my father hired you. Start there," I said, trying to control my frustration but knowing it was not working.

"What do you remember about your parents?" he asked me. "Nothing. I don't remember them at all," I replied. "Aurora, you were five, almost six, when you went to live with your grandparents. How do you not remember anything?" he asked me. I had thought about this before. From the day I first stepped into my grandparents' farmhouse, I had no memory of anything before. At five, I should have remembered something. Anything. But my life before that day was a blank.

I shook my head at David. "I don't remember anything before that day. The day I went to live with my grandparents," I told him. "I can only see my parents' faces in the pictures that my grandparents had in their house. Those, and the dreams," I said quietly. The dreams of my parents I would prefer to have done without. They were more like nightmares.

"You have dreams about your parents?" David asked me. I heard the surprise in his voice. I stood from my chair and took a few steps across the room. "Nightmares really," I said quietly, looking over at David. "What are these dreams about?" he asked. I was hesitant to answer as it was not something I liked to remember. I had never told anyone about the dreams before, not even my grandparents.

"They always start with my parents and me together. In the end, I always see them dead and I am running. People are after me and I have to get away. There are trees and it's dark. I am running, but it seems that they will catch me. And then I am falling. I always fall, and it seems I am falling forever. When I stop falling, someone grabs me, and then I wake up," I said, realizing I was pacing the room as I spoke. I stopped and turned towards David.

"It's buried in your subconscious," David said calmly, and I gave him a funny look. "That is very close to what happened, but your father was not there. It was just your mother and you. Men came after you and they killed your mother, but you got away. You ran. They did chase after you and you were running through a wooded area. It was dark and you didn't see the cliff. You fell over the side, but it was all dirt and was sloped, so you pretty much slid down the side of the cliff," he told me.

Chapter 3

I watched him intently as he spoke, and his eyes never left mine. "You were semi-unconscious at the bottom of the cliff when you were found. The men never found you in the dark. They made it to the cliff but could not see to the bottom of it because it was nighttime. Your father found you and that is when he brought you to Kansas," he told me. I shook my head.

"No, that can't be right," I whispered. "My father is dead. He wouldn't have left me," I continued, feeling my eyes fill with tears. "Why? Why did someone kill my mother. Why would they be after me? It doesn't make any sense. My grandparents…" I said in alarm.

"They are not your grandparents," David said softly. I gasped and choked on a sob. I could not breathe, and I bent forward putting my hands on my knees. David jumped from the couch and I felt his hands on my back, rubbing, soothing. "Relax, Aurora. Slow breaths. Concentrate on inhaling and exhaling and calming down," I heard him say.

I felt the air rush into my lungs, and I choked. I concentrated on David's words and I tried to focus on taking normal breaths. When I was finally inhaling and exhaling in a steady rhythm, I stood up and looked at David. The tears were still rolling down my cheeks. I inhaled deeply, glad that I could finally breathe normal again. The only time this ever happened to me was when I thought about my parents, or when I was in the dark. For some reason, I was deathly afraid of the dark.

"I'm sorry," he said gently. His voice was incredibly soft but sincere. "Who am I? My whole life was a lie. Why can't I remember?" I asked him, realizing that everything I knew was fake. Everything my grandparents had told me was a lie. They were not even my grandparents. David took my hand and led me to the couch that he had been sitting on. Then he sat down beside me.

"Your name is Aurora, but your last name is Davis, not Simpson. The couple that raised you, the Simpsons, knew your father. They agreed to take you and raise you in order to protect you. The people that killed your mother want you dead as well," he said, and my eyes flew open wide. "But why?" I asked him.

"I think that they believe you know who killed your mother and that you could implicate them," he replied. I could only shake my head. I had no idea who had killed my mother. I did not even remember her. Then I thought about what David had said. My dreams. They were only part dream and part memory. But in my dreams, I never saw anyone but my parents. And now, David told me that my father was not even there.

"Where's my father?" I asked him, still unsure if I wanted to believe everything that he was telling me. "Your father is in prison for the murder of your mother," he told me. My hand flew to my mouth. I could tell by the look in his eyes that he was being honest. There were so many more questions running through my head.

"But why? Why didn't he think I knew who killed my mother? Why did he leave me with strangers? If he didn't kill her, why is he in prison?" I asked, and the questions continued to fall from my mouth. None of this made any sense to me. When I finally stopped talking and asking questions, I looked over at David. He had to have answers for me. I needed to know.

"Your father went to prison to protect you," he said gently. "The people you call your grandparents knew that you had been traumatized by your experience. They knew that you had no memory of what had happened. You were the only one who could prove he was innocent, but you did not remember anything. He had to hide you to keep you safe," he explained.

"So, he has been in prison for nineteen years?" I asked in alarm. I had just turned twenty-four and had moved in with my grandparents, or whoever they were, when I was five. David nodded. "He was set up," he told me. I looked down at my hands in my lap. "So, now what?" I asked softly. "Now we have to make you remember," he told me. I looked up at him in surprise.

"How? How can I just remember? I haven't remembered for nineteen years. I can't just make myself remember," I told him anxiously. David stood from the couch and looked down at me. "I'll be right back," he said and walked towards a hallway on the far side of the living room.

He was only gone a few minutes, but he returned with a box in his hands. He set the box down on the table in front of the couch, and then he sat down beside me once again. I watched as he opened it and started pulling out stacks of papers, some files, and some books that looked like journals. When the box was empty, he set it on the floor and looked at me.

"This is not going to be easy for you," he said, and I glanced down at the stacks of papers. "This is everything about what happened the night your mother was killed. You need to go through it. Reading what really happened and seeing it again may trigger your memories of that night," he told me. I felt my body shudder and wondered what all I would find in the stacks of papers and books on the table.

David reached for the newspaper that was sitting on top. He handed it to me, and I saw a picture of my mother and father on the front. Then I read the title of the article. "Colorado Politician and Tycoon Arrested for Murder of Wife and Daughter." I looked up at David in surprise. "Read the article," he told me gently.

I looked down again and started to read. The article said that my father, Arthur Davis, had killed both my mother and me in a fit of rage. It explained that my parents were having marital problems and it was rumored that he had killed both of us because he was having an affair. He killed us so that he could be with this other woman.

"I don't understand. If everyone thinks I am dead, why is someone after me?" I asked him. "Because your body was never found, your father was never convicted of your death. But also, because your body was never found, whoever did this has assumed that you are still alive. They knew that they killed your mother, but they also know that the police never found you that night. They have been looking for you ever since," he told me.

I reached for the next paper on the stack. It was a police report with a description of what they found when they arrived at the scene of my mother's murder. After I read through it, I reached for a folder that was on top of another stack. David reached out and put his hand over mine before I could pick it up. I looked up at him.

"These are photos," he said, and I knew he meant crime scene photos. I nodded up at him and reached again for the file. I set it in my lap and just looked at it for a few moments. Taking a couple of deep breaths, I opened the folder and looked down at the picture that was on top.

It was straight out of my dream and my hand flew up to cover my mouth. It was a picture of my mother lying on the ground. Blood had pooled around her body and her eyes were open but not looking at anything. It was the same way I saw her in my dreams. The only difference was that my father was not beside her. I felt the tears in my eyes once more as I reached out and touched the photo.

My grandparents had never told me how my parents had died. It was too hard to think of them as anything other than my grandparents, even though now, I knew that they were not. I could not look past the photo in front of me, and my hands shook as I touched it. I finally closed the folder, unable to look at the photo any longer. The sobs wracked my body and I was overcome with feelings of despair and loss knowing that my dreams were not just dreams.

I felt David's arms reach around me and pull me against him, and I did not have the strength to resist. He held me tightly and rubbed my back while I cried for everything that I had lost. Nineteen years of my life had been a lie and I remembered nothing of the five, almost six years before that. The only thing I could remember about my parents was that my mother was dead, and up until today, I had thought my father was as well.

I cried for a long time and David just held me. When I finally felt the tears subsiding, I knew I had no tears left. When I stopped crying, I did not have the energy to sit up and David kept his arms around me as I laid against his chest. My whole body hurt from the turmoil, and I felt an ache in my chest.

"I'm sorry," I heard David whisper softly. I nodded against his chest, thankful that he was still holding me. He had told me the truth, and I did not think I could handle being alone right now. I wondered how I had been able to forget what had happened to my mother. I guess as a five-year-old child, my mind just could not handle it. It disturbed me that I had forgotten my own parents.

When David finally released me, I sat up. I looked down at the folder in my lap but could not bring myself to open it again. David stood and I looked up at him. "Let's get some lunch," he said. He was giving me a distraction and I was grateful. "I don't really have anything to eat in the house since I have been in Salina for a couple weeks now, but I will order us something and have it delivered," he continued.

"Chinese or pizza?" he asked me with a smile. "Pizza," I told him, managing a bit of a smile in return. "You got it," he said, and pulled out his phone. Thirty minutes later there was a knock on the door, and David walked back into the room with two pizza boxes. I followed him as he walked into the kitchen.

He took two plates out of the cabinet and filled two glasses with ice water. We sat down at the bar where he had set the boxes of pizza. He grabbed a plate and put a couple of slices on it and set it in front of me. I took a bite not even realizing how hungry I had been. We ate in silence for a few minutes. "So, you are not really a writer, are you?" I asked him, taking another bite.

"I really am," he said, and I looked up at him in surprise. "I'm a reporter. Your dad read some of my work and sent me a letter. He claimed he was innocent and wanted to know if I would come and talk to him. I could not resist interviewing a murderer, so I readily agreed. He did not tell me everything at first, but enough that I was interested in getting the whole story," he told me.

"So, he hired you to write his story?" I asked him. "No, he hired me to find the truth. He did not tell me about you at first. Not until I believed that he was innocent. But once he told me about you, I promised him that I would watch out for you. That was two years ago," he replied. My eyes widened in surprise.

"You've been watching me for two years?" I asked him in astonishment. He nodded. "I never came into the restaurant until I saw the men following you. I needed to talk to you and try to get you used to me. I needed to gain your trust in case something like this happened," he replied honestly.

This whole situation was overwhelming me. My whole world had just been flipped upside down. My dad was alive and in prison, and someone wanted me dead. I needed answers as well, and I knew that David was the only one that could help me get to the answers I needed. Somehow, we had to prove my father did not kill my mother. I needed to remember.

I stood from the bar and walked back into the living room and sat down on the couch. I reached for the file that held the crime scene photos. David followed me and reached down and covered my hand with his once again. I looked up at him. "Are you sure about this?" he asked me softly. I nodded and he released my hand.

I lifted the folder and set it in my lap. Slowly, I opened it and saw the picture of my mother. Then I moved the photo to the bottom of the stack and went through the rest of the photos. I studied each one carefully, hoping it would trigger something in my memory. Some of the pictures reminded me of dreams that I had had, but nothing triggered a memory.

Chapter 4

David and I spent the next two hours going through the stacks of papers and pictures. He had every news article that had been written about my mother's murder and my disappearance, plus several journals that he had written during interviews with my father. I did not open any of the journals, but I did go through all the news stories. I also browsed through articles that covered my father's trial and sentencing.

It was a weird kind of déjà vu as I thought about the similarities between my dreams and what had really happened to my mother. I also could not yet evaluate what I was feeling about finding out that my father was alive. I had believed he was dead for nineteen years. Now I found out he was sitting in prison and I knew he would stay there until I could remember. At least now I knew why he had never come for me.

Remembering was just the first part. Even if I could remember who killed my mother, how did we get my father out of jail? How did we get the evidence to convict the person that did it? Would my father and I be safe once he was out of jail? Those were the questions I needed answers to now.

I put the last article down on the table and sighed in frustration. I leaned back against the couch. David reached over and patted my hand in my lap. "You will remember. It's locked in there somewhere," he said, pointing at my head. "Let's say I do remember. Then what? How do we get my dad out of jail? I mean, nineteen years after his conviction, am I supposed to just walk into the prison and say someone else did it and they will release him? I really don't think it works that way," I said, hearing the frustration in my own voice.

David reached down to the table and picked up the stack of journals. "You need to read these," he said softly. "You will find a lot of the answers you are looking for in here," he told me. He laid the journals on my lap and I laid my hand on the top one. I closed my eyes for a moment and searched for a memory of when I was five. Blank!

"Since we don't know how long we will be here, I'm going to make a trip to the grocery store," David said standing. I nodded up at him but could not speak. He gave me a tender smile, then headed into the kitchen and to the garage. I looked down at the stack of journals again and took a couple of deep breaths. Then I opened the cover of the first one and started to read. It began two years ago.

Journal Entry June 5, 2018

I am getting ready to go visit Arthur Davis. He requested an interview with me, and I could not resist. He is claiming that he is innocent of the murder of his wife and daughter seventeen years ago and wants to tell me his story. Most of the people in prison claim innocence, but I am going into this interview with an open mind. I have already researched everything I could about his trial and sentencing. Originally, he was charged with the murder of his five-year-old daughter, Aurora, but no body had ever been found so those charges were dropped. I will go and listen to his story. If I find any truth to it, I will have to look into this matter more. However, I am not expecting much.

Arthur Davis looks nothing like the man he was before going to prison, when he was a rich politician. His face is now covered in a full beard and his body is toned, although slender. I see hard lines in his face that were not there before. Prison definitely changes a man. He wants to begin at the beginning and that is how I prefer it. The beginning for this story starts with his marriage to Abigail.

Arthur Davis was a successful businessman with his hand in politics. He met Abigail at a Christmas fundraising event. She was Abigail Smaldone at the time, and her father was Vincent Smaldone. They were distance relatives of the crime underlord Clarence Smaldone. Vincent had kept his nose clean and gotten into politics.

Vincent's son, Jimmy, was the current owner of several casinos in the Denver area. Jimmy and Abigail, although brother and sister, never got along well. When Arthur Davis met Abigail for the first time, he set his sights on her. He called it love at first sight, but it took a while to convince Abigail that he was the right man for her.

When Abigail and Arthur started dating, it caused waves in the Smaldone family. Arthur was becoming a political icon in the community, and Vincent Smaldone was not happy about having the competition. Arthur had been warned on more than one occasion to leave Abigail alone, but he hired private security instead. When they married, neither Vincent nor Jimmy attended the wedding.

Several of Arthur's businesses were set on fire shortly after their marriage, but with the insurance money, he rebuilt them. The newspapers highlighted the attacks against Arthur and that made his popularity grow. The people of Colorado loved both Arthur and Abigail, and they were the love match of the decade.

Arthur donated funds to local community projects and Abigail volunteered at community functions, becoming an icon for youth in the Denver area. She was on the board of directors for several charitable organizations. She spent time in community centers and food kitchens, and she was instrumental in streamlining a couple of the non-profits in the area to better reach more people with their resources. Both Arthur and Abigail were in the news frequently for their donations of time, money, and resources to the community.

When Abigail got pregnant, the people of the community followed her pregnancy with great interest. It was as if she were royalty. When she gave birth to a baby girl, newspapers flew off the shelf. People wanted to know if it was a boy or girl and what the baby's name was. Neither Abigail nor Arthur were shy in front of the camera, and with new baby Aurora, she was soon in the spotlight as well.

Together, Arthur, Abigail, and Aurora were living the American dream. When rumors of marital problems began a few years later, no one knew who started it. The three of them continued to appear in public together to try and dispel the rumors. Then rumors of an affair began to circulate.

Arthur adamantly refuted those claims, but when a young woman showed up claiming to be his mistress, doubt had been planted. According to Arthur, Abigail never believed the rumors. Arthur said that Abigail was the only one that mattered to him. If she believed him, that was all he cared about.

The woman claimed that she knew Arthur from high school and that they had dated for a time. Arthur admitted to me that this was true. However, the woman claimed that they had been sexually involved for over six months at the time she came forward. Arthur was successful in discrediting her, but it took several months.

During this time, Abigail willingly spoke to any reporters that approached her. They all noticed the security that followed her, and she explained to them that her family was trying to discredit her husband and she claimed they had been behind the rumors. I found evidence of this in different news reports where Abigail had given a statement to the press. She explained that her family had not wanted her to marry Arthur due to the political competition between her husband and father.

Journal Entry June 12, 2018

Arthur hired security for Abigail, and they went with her any time she was in public. They both knew it was her family that had started the trouble, and they both acted like the rumors had no effect on them. The only time that security had not followed Abigail was when she went to the hair salon before a gala event that they were to attend.

When the carnival came to town, Aurora had seen it in the newspaper. She was five years old at the time and had begged both Arthur and Abigail to take her. On the day they decided to go, Arthur was supposed to have been there with Abigail and Aurora. A phone meeting had come up at the last minute and Arthur was unable to attend. He told Aurora that if his meeting ended early, then he would meet them there.

I stopped reading there. The carnival had been the last dream I had. The one where my parents were both killed. I could not get the image out of my head, especially now that I had seen the crime scene photos. My mother, lying in a pool of blood. Her eyes open, but lifeless. I could see that picture even when my eyes were open now. My nightmares had become reality.

I closed the journal and stood from the couch. Did my mother's family have her killed? All because she married my father? It seemed ludicrous, but I had never met them. I knew there were evil people out there, but I grew up in a small town where the worst trouble people got into were DUI's.

According to the journals, and to my father, my mother's family was related to crime lords and corruption. Those kinds of people were ruthless and hurt people all the time. I did not want a part in any of this. I just wanted my life back. But then there was my father. He is currently sitting in prison for killing my mother, and supposedly he did not do it. What if he did?

That would not explain those two men in the café this morning. They were definitely after me, but why? Were they trying to kill me to shut me up? They would have to know I did not remember anything, otherwise, I would have spoken up long before now and gotten my father out of prison already, or at least I would have tried.

I sat back down on the couch and closed my eyes, leaning against the back of the couch. What if I never remembered? What was going to happen to me? I needed to talk to my father. I needed to see him. Now, I just needed David to return so I could convince him of this.

I looked around in amazement at all the carnival lights. My mother held my hand and smiled down at me as we stood in line for a hot dog. She asked me what rides I wanted to ride, and I grinned up at her. It was cool outside, but my hand was warm in hers. We got our hot dogs and walked to a table and sat down.

I noticed the two men that were following us. They stood beside us at the table as we ate. I watched them as they watched the people around us. They never spoke a word to us, but I was not afraid of them. They were familiar. When we were done eating, we headed towards the tilt-a-whirl. It was my favorite ride.

We got seated inside the open car and I could not keep the smile from my face. I was so excited for the ride to start. "Do you want to spin fast?" my mother asked in an animated tone. I grinned up at her and nodded. The car began to move and we both laughed as we pulled on the circle table in front of us and the car spun faster. When the ride came to a stop, I looked up at my mother. "Can we do it again?" I asked her. She laughed and agreed.

We exited the ride and went to stand in the line again. Suddenly, my mother pulled on my hand. She was pulling me away from the ride, and quickly. "Aurora, we need to run," she said, and I saw the fear in her eyes. We headed towards the trees that bordered the field where the rides were set up. The two men that always followed us were nowhere to be seen. Suddenly, my mother dropped my hand and fell to the ground.

"Mommy!" I cried, as I saw the pool of blood spreading out around her. "Run, Aurora," she whispered. I looked up and saw the men approaching. When I looked back down, my mother was motionless, and her eyes were wide open. I turned and ran towards the trees as fast as I could. The branches tore at my clothes and hair. It was dark, and I could not see very far in front of me with just pinpricks of light from the moon shining through.

I could hear the men behind me. They were calling my name. I kept running until suddenly I was falling. I screamed. Then I felt a hand go over my mouth and I struggled against whoever was holding me. "Aurora! Aurora! Wake up!" I heard and felt the hands on my shoulders shaking me.

My eyes flew open and I gasped for breath, choking on the sob in my throat. David. My eyes met his and I grasped his hands that were on my shoulders. I could not stop the flow of tears. He sat down beside me and pulled me against his chest. Feeling his arms around

me made me feel safe, and for some reason, that made me
cry harder.

Chapter 5

When my tears finally subsided, I pulled away from David and leaned back against the couch. I closed my eyes for a moment and tried to breathe deeply. When my breathing evened out, I opened my eyes and looked at David. He was watching me and waiting.

"It was different this time," I told him. "My father wasn't there. My mom told me to run. There were two men following me through the trees." I stopped there, trying to recall the details of the dream. "Had you ever seen those men before?" David asked, and I shook my head. They were not familiar to me at all. That made me think of something else.

"No, but there were two other men. When we were eating, they were standing by us. Following us around the carnival," I said. "But I am pretty sure they came there with us. I wasn't afraid of them. They have never been in my dream before," I said, and David nodded. "That was your hired security. Both of them were killed as well, while you and your mother were riding the ride," he said. I looked up at David.

"But how does my remembering help us? It was two men I have never seen before, or at least, I don't remember them. No one is going to believe me that it wasn't my father. He has already been convicted. My dreams are not going to be considered valid evidence," I told him, once again feeling defeated.

"No, but it's a start. We now know for sure it wasn't your father. We just have to find the evidence," he said. I looked at him in confusion. "It happened nineteen years ago. There isn't going to be any evidence," I replied, hearing the hopelessness in my voice. I dropped my head into my hands.

"You must have forgotten that I am a reporter. It is my job to investigate. This could be the biggest story of my career if we can get your father's conviction overturned," he told me. I stood abruptly and crossed my arms over my chest, staring down at him. "You want to use me for a story? To advance your career?" I asked in alarm.

David stood and took a step towards me. "Aurora, this was not my idea. Your father has hired me to do this. He wants the story to be made public. He wants the truth to be found and he wants everyone to know it. I have agreed to that. I also told him that I would keep you safe and that is what I intend to do," he replied.

I could not be upset anymore. David and I were in this together. We just had to find a place to start. "So, what do we do now?" I asked him. "Now we go to Colorado," he said gently. "But first, we are going to rest here for a couple of days. I picked you up some clothes. I hope they fit," he continued, pointing at a couple bags on the floor next to the chair.

"Come on," he said. "Let me show you to your room." He picked up the bags and headed down the hallway. With no other choices, I followed him. He opened a door and stepped inside. It was a typical bedroom. Bed, dresser, chair, closet. Nothing extravagant, but it looked comfortable.

David set the bags on the bed and pointed out the bathroom across the hall. "Why don't you go through those clothes, take a shower, and I'll fix something for dinner. A shower might help you relax," he said. He was probably right. I definitely was feeling extremely tense right now.

I rummaged through the bags and pulled out some clothes. David did a surprisingly good job of judging my size. When I stepped into the shower, I stood under the water and let it beat on my back for a while. I tried not to think of anything, but that was hard considering my life had been torn upside down just before breakfast. I did not know what to think or what to feel.

Suddenly, an image of my mother filled my head. She was elegantly dressed and standing by a wide staircase. She knelt down in front of me and gave me a hug. "Now you be good and go to bed on time. Your father and I will see you in the morning," she said. Then she leaned forward and gave me a hug and kissed my cheek.

I felt a hand in mine and looked up to see Annie smiling down at me. Annie was my caretaker when my parents were not home. I loved Annie like a second mother. She was exceedingly kind and she played games with me. I knew she would let me stay up a little longer than my bedtime was supposed to be.

I looked back at my mother and saw my father approach. He gave my mother a kiss and then lifted me into his arms. I wrapped my arms around his neck and hugged him. "Okay, squirt, I know you will be good while we are gone. So, we will see you in the morning," he said, lowering me to the floor.

When they left, Annie and I had played hide-and-seek. The house was huge, and I had gone into my father's office and hid under his desk. I could not remember if Annie had found me or if I had come out of hiding on my own. The rest of the memory was gone. I wondered what had happened to Annie after my mother was killed and my father was sent to prison.

I finished my shower, knowing the tears were falling but the water from the shower washed them away. When I was dressed, I looked in the mirror. All signs of the tears were gone. I walked down the hallway towards the living room and could smell food cooking. I wondered if David knew how to cook. Ready or not, I was about to find out.

David kept the conversation during dinner neutral and I was grateful. We talked about our favorite movies, actors and actresses. Then we talked about our favorite music and bands. The food was really good, and I did not mean to sound so surprised when I told David that. He just laughed.

After dinner, I helped him clean up the kitchen. I was exhausted after getting little sleep the night before. The nap I had taken earlier had not been restful. David must have been reading my mind because the next thing he said was that we should call it a night. I agreed and headed to my bedroom.

I realized I did not have anything but t-shirts to sleep in, but I was okay with that. Crawling into bed, I sighed, grateful that the day was over. I closed my eyes and thought about the only memory I had of my parents, other than the dreams. I could easily see my mother in her elegant dress and my father in his suit. I fell asleep quickly with a smile on my face.

I was five years old. I was walking with my mother down the street. We were headed to the hair salon. My mother had parked the car at the closest spot to the salon, but it was still a block away. I did not get a lot of time with my mother alone, so I was glad she was letting me come with her. Even if it was just the hair salon.

I had never been inside a salon before, and I looked around in awe as we stepped inside. We walked up to a counter and my mom gave her name to the lady standing behind it. We both took a seat in the waiting area. My mother smiled down at me and I thought she was beautiful.

When a lady called my mother's name, my mother told me to stay sitting in the seat I was in until she was done. The lady that had called my mother's name told her that it was okay to bring me back with her. My mother looked over at me and reached her hand out to me. I jumped down from the chair and ran to her, slipping my hand into hers.

We were led to a large room in back where salon chairs were positioned along both of the side walls. The nice lady told me to have a seat in the chair next to the one my mom sat down in. I watched with keen interest as the woman started doing my mother's hair. They were both talking the whole time and sometimes they would ask me questions. I felt very grown up and happy.

When my mother was done, I climbed down from the tall chair and put my hand into my mother's once more. We walked to the front of the salon and my mother paid the lady who had done her hair. Then we turned towards the door. We stepped out into the sunshine, and it took a few seconds for my eyes to adjust to the brightness. We turned and started walking towards the car.

All of a sudden, I felt strong arms grab me and I was being lifted from the ground. "Mommy!" I screamed and looked around in desperation for her. I saw another man with his hand firmly on my mother's arm, pulling her towards the street. The large man who held me followed them. I beat on the man that held me, but he easily grabbed my wrists and held them down.

A long black car waited in the street and the other man opened the door and pushed my mother inside. As we approached the car, the man set me in the car on the seat next to my mother and closed the door behind me. Then the car started moving down the road.

I looked up at my mom to see if she was as scared as I was. She put her arm around me and pulled me against her, giving me a small smile. It helped me relax just a bit until I looked around the car and saw the two men sitting in the seat across from us. They looked really scary.

The older man was watching me, and he had a smile on his face. I was not sure what to think, so I looked up at my mother once more. Then the man spoke. "Aurora, I am glad to finally meet you," the older man said. I looked back at him and wondered who he was and why we were sitting in his car.

"Aurora, do you know who I am?" the older man asked. I could not speak, and I leaned farther into my mother's side as I shook my head. I felt her arm tighten around me even more. "I am your grandfather. Your mother is my daughter," he said in a gentle tone. I looked up at my mother, but there was no smile on her face when she nodded to confirm this was true.

"Aurora, dear, come here and let me look at you," he said, and opened his arms out to me. "No," I heard my mother say, her hold on me tightening even more, almost hurting me. Then I saw the younger man reach into his suit jacket and pull out a gun. My eyes opened wide and I buried my face into my mother's side.

"Jimmy, there is no need for that. Put the gun away," the older man said. I snuck a peak at the two men and saw the one called Jimmy put the gun away. The older man was still smiling at me. "Aurora, no one is going to hurt you. Come here, please. I just want to see how you have grown," he said in a soft and kind voice.

I felt my mother's arm loosen from around me and she gave me a gentle nudge. I was small enough that I could stand up in the car, so I slid from the seat and walked the short distance to the older man until I was standing in front of him. He reached out and lifted my hands and pulled me a step closer until I was standing just between his knees. He did not lower my hands but just looked at me as I looked back at him.

I did not know what to do or say, so I stood quiet and motionless. "You look just like your mother when she was your age," he said gently. I noticed the splattering of gray in his hair and the creases at the sides of his eyes.

"Do you go to school yet?" he asked me. I shook my head. "I just turned five," I told him quietly.

He nodded then looked past me to my mother. He did not say anything to her but looked back at me. "I think you should come and visit me some time," he said. Then he pointed at the man beside him. "This is your Uncle Jimmy. He has a daughter about your age. I bet you two would get along well together. Would you like to meet her sometime?" he asked me. I just nodded, unsure if I would like that or not.

"Well, I would love for you to come and visit me. Jimmy would love it too. You can call me Grandpa Vic. That's what Jimmy's daughter calls me," he told me. Then he slid over a bit and indicated for me to sit between the two of them. I hesitantly sat down and now was looking across at my mother. Her eyes were open wide, and she seemed afraid as she watched me intently.

I jumped down from the seat and ran to her. I threw my arms around her and she wrapped me in her arms and held me tightly. The next thing I knew, the car stopped, and the door opened. My mother set me out of the car, but she did not follow me quite yet. I could hear voices inside the car and when my mother stepped out, there were tears rolling down her face.

She grabbed my hand and pulled me to the sidewalk in front of the salon. Then we headed to the car once again. My mother's grip on my hand was like steel, and I had to run to keep up with her. When we got to the car, she opened my door and I got in. She did not say a word to me until we got home.

"Go with Annie, dear. I have to talk to your father," my mother said. I ran to Annie and she lifted me in her arms. She moved quickly up the stairs. I did not see either of my parents that evening and I ate my dinner in the sitting room outside of my bedroom. It was just Annie and me, but I was okay with that. I had been scared today, and this was my safe place.

Chapter 6

When I woke up the next morning, I sat up and looked around. I was in David's house. The dream had been so real, and as I thought about it, I knew that it was a memory. I could still picture my grandfather's face, and the tears that my mother had cried. I could not stop the tears from falling as I remembered my mother and I remembered that now she was gone.

I did not hear my door open, and I did not hear David enter the room until he sat down on the bed beside me. He reached around me and held me against him as I cried. He did not say anything, but he just held me. I felt safe like this, even though I knew that I was not.

When the tears finally subsided, David pulled away from me. I looked up at him. "Was it another dream?" he asked me. I shook my head. "It was a memory," I whispered, recalling my mother's face once more. "I'll be right back," he said. Then he stood from the bed and walked out of the room.

When he returned, he walked towards me with something in his hands. He held it out to me. It was a journal similar to the ones that he had written my father's story in. "I don't think I can handle reading any more right now," I told him honestly. He flipped through the pages and I saw that they were all blank. I looked up at him in confusion.

"I want you to write down anything and everything you remember. Every little detail," he told me. I reached out and took the journal and the pen from him. I needed to do this while it was still fresh in my mind. I nodded at David and opened the book and started writing. I did not even hear him leave the room or shut the door behind him.

I wrote down everything I could remember about that time with my grandfather. I described both him and my Uncle Jimmy as well as I could remember. I described the black gun that Jimmy had pulled out and the gray that was splattered through my grandfather's hair. I described the look of fear in my mother's eyes and the look of desperation when she got out of the car crying.

When I was finished, I wrote about the memory of my mother and father dressed for an elegant evening. I described the dress my mother wore, the suit that my father had on, and the wide staircase they were standing beside. The more I wrote, the more I remembered, describing my bedroom and the games that Annie and I had played that evening when my parents left. Then I described Annie. Something about Annie nagged at me, but I did not know what it was.

I finally put the journal down and got dressed. When I walked out of the bedroom and into the kitchen, David handed me a cup of coffee then turned back to the breakfast he was fixing. I sat down at the table and sipped my coffee. All I could think about were my new memories that were actually memories from nineteen years ago.

"Will you let me read it?" I heard David ask softly, turning to look at me. I knew he meant the journal and what I had written. "It's the memory of a five-year-old," I told him. "I know," he replied softly, giving me a hint of a smile. I just nodded back at him.

After breakfast, I went and got the journal from my room. I handed it to David, and he sat down on the couch to read. Washing the dishes from breakfast would distract me from the fact that he was reading about my life. When I was done, I walked back into the living room. David sat on the couch with the journal closed on his lap.

"Come here," he said, patting the seat beside him. I could not read the expression on his face. I walked towards the couch and sat down. David handed me his phone. When I looked down at the screen, I saw it was a news article about my parents. There was a picture of them in the same elegant clothing that I remembered. They were both smiling, and my father was shaking a man's hand.

I quickly read through the article and about the gala that they had attended that evening. When I was finished reading, I scrolled back up to the picture and looked at my parents. This was how I now remembered them. Happy. After a few more minutes, I handed the phone back to David. "Thank you," I told him softly.

"There's more," he said, but I did not like the expression on his face. Whatever it was would not be good. When he handed me back the phone, there was another article that he had pulled up. I read through it quickly, feeling the gasp as I inhaled sharply, and my hand flew to my mouth. Annie.

While my parents were at the gala, someone broke into our house and killed Annie. But what about me? Where was I when they killed her? Was I in bed and they just left me alone? I knew that was not true. I was not sure how I knew, but I knew. Closing my eyes tightly, I pictured Annie how I remembered her.

Suddenly, I remembered a dark place. I was hiding. Annie and I played hide-and-seek a lot. It had been my favorite game, but I did not like the dark. I knew I was scared of the dark and would never have hidden in a dark place. Putting my hands out in front of me, I could feel the curved wall. It curved around in front of me in a half circle, just barely large enough for me to hide behind and have a little room to move. The wall behind me was flat against my back.

I could hear Annie's voice telling me to not come out for any reason and to stay quiet. "Don't make a sound," she said. I remembered closing my eyes tightly so

I would not notice the darkness around me. Then I heard gunshots. My hands flew to my mouth to stifle my sobs. I had to remain quiet. Whoever was out there would find me if I made a sound.

I could hear breaking glass and furniture scraping across the floor. Then I heard voices. "She's not here," one man said. "She's got to be here. I want her found!" another man said, and I recognized the voice. It was my grandfather's voice. He had killed Annie. I remained silent and hidden until the house was quiet, but still I did not come out.

I could hear sirens in the distance and a little while later I heard voices again. My legs were shaking from standing for so long and I still held my eyes tightly closed. Suddenly, the curved wall in front of me moved forward and I was falling. Strong hands lifted me, and I screamed and kicked. The room was too bright for me to open my eyes and I had to keep them tightly closed.

Then I heard my father's voice in my ear and his hand on my back rubbing gently. I cried and wrapped my arms around his neck, holding him with his suit jacket clenched in my fists. "You're safe, Aurora," I heard through my sobs. I clung to him, afraid to let go. Afraid that whoever had been here would come back for me.

My father started walking, but I could not open my eyes because of the light. We entered a room, but I could tell he did not turn the light on. He sat down and held me on his lap with his arm still around me. "Aurora, you can open your eyes now," he said softly. I slowly opened my eyes and let my eyes adjust to the dim light in the room. Then I looked up at my father.

I opened my eyes in alarm and looked over at David. "They were after me!" I exclaimed. "The men that killed Annie, they were after me. I heard my grandfather's voice. He wanted me," I said, choking on the last part. David took my hand in his and nodded.

"That was not the first time they tried to get you," he said, and my jaw dropped. "According to your father, they tried to get you from the hospital after you were first born," he told me. "But what did they want from me?" I asked him.

"What do they still want from you is the right question. The men at the café are your grandfather's men, or maybe your uncle's. I'm not sure," he continued. "The more you can remember, the better. Write it down," he said gently, handing me the journal. It took me a long time to write about that experience. I had to close my eyes and remember the darkness. Then I could focus on the sounds and the voices that I had heard. At least now I knew why I was scared of the dark.

Before going to bed that evening, David told me that we would be leaving in the morning. We were going to Colorado. I was apprehensive just thinking about it. Why were we going to the one place they could find me? I had asked David this question. His response was because that is where the answers were and that is the last place that they would expect me to go.

Crying myself to sleep seemed to become the new normal for me. The strange thing about that is I could not even remember the last time I had cried, until I met David. I thought about my parents as I lay in bed. My mother was gone, and somehow, for the last nineteen years, I had forgotten her. My father might as well be gone since he was sitting in prison. David had already told me that I could not go and see him. It was too dangerous.

I had no idea what type of answers we were looking for or how we were supposed to find any. Going to Colorado just did not make sense to me, but David assured me that we needed to go. Somehow, I managed to fall asleep, but I tossed and turned with flashes of memories and nightmares waking me up frequently.

Chapter 7

The next morning, I pulled myself from the bed and showered, hoping it would help wake me up. Unfortunately, it did not help much. I headed towards the kitchen, grateful for the smell of coffee that was leading me there. David poured me a cup and set it on the table. I sat down and lifted the cup to my mouth and took a drink.

"You didn't sleep well," David said, turning and looking at me. I just shook my head. I was not in the mood to talk about what I was feeling right now. David must have sensed that because he did not say anything else as he set two plates on the table and sat down across from me. We ate in silence, but that was just as awkward.

After breakfast, we washed the dishes together. When the last dish was put away, David stepped in front of me and put his hands on my shoulders. I looked up at him. "Aurora, we have to find answers. We have to go," he said softly. "I know," I whispered. Then he pulled me against his chest and wrapped his arms around me.

No one had held me like this since my father when I was five. It felt secure and I felt safe. I smelled the aftershave that David wore, and it was familiar. He had held me while I cried, and now the scent was familiar to me. I felt his hand run down my hair and his other hand rubbing my back. I wish I could feel like this all the time, but I knew it was not going to happen.

Slowly, I took a step back from David and looked up at him. His eyes were intense as he watched me, and I realized that he was the only person in my life right now. I had no one else. He was it. I trusted him, and my father trusted him. For now, that would have to be enough for me.

However, the look he had in his eyes right now was one that I recognized. He wanted me, and I did not know how I felt about that. I remembered back in the café when he first started coming in. I had been attracted to him immediately. Every once in a while, he would engage me in conversation, and I remembered wondering if he was interested. I also remembered telling Chelsea that I would be glad to go out with him.

Circumstances were different now. He had been there to watch me. He had been looking out for me because my father had asked him to. There had been secrets kept from me, and I knew that I did not even know them all. The one thing I did know was that I felt safe in David's arms. I could not help myself from stepping towards him and wrapping my arms around him once more.

I felt his arms come around me and his chin lowered until it rested on my head. "I would never hurt you, Aurora," he whispered just over my ear. I knew it was the truth, and I knew I had nothing to fear from him. I held onto him for a few more minutes before finally stepping away again. I looked up at him. "Let's go," I said.

David grabbed our two bags and took them to the car. I followed right behind him and got in. He put our bags in the trunk, then got in. He started the car and looked over at me. The smile on his face drew out a smile from me. I still did not know what our plan was when we got to Colorado, but I did not ask. It was more than I wanted to think about right now.

It only took about ten minutes for us to reach the interstate. We headed north on I-135. It would take us about eight hours to get to Denver. I asked David about his career in journalism. He surprised me by telling me not only did he write for the local newspaper in Wichita, but he also wrote for several magazines and had written several biographies based on interviews he had done with people in prison. He wrote about their lives and how their choices had led them to a life of crime.

He explained that my father had read several of his books from the prison library and then did some research on David before contacting him. My father would not have just trusted anyone. I knew this now, and that is why I knew I could trust David.

David had packed up the box with the newspaper articles and the journals he had written. The box sat on the back seat. I had both my journal and the journal of David's that I had started reading, with me. I figured a long car ride would be a perfect time to read some more.

I held the two journals in my lap as David and I talked. Neither of us had any idea how long we would be together and hiding out, so it was natural that we learn about each other. I told him about the farmhouse I grew up in and about the two people who had raised me. I would always see them as my grandparents. They had loved me as if I were their granddaughter.

David had grown up in Wichita and got his degree in journalism from Kansas State University. Writing was all he had ever wanted to do. He must be fairly good at it to be so successful. He told me about his college days and about some of the stories he had written over the last few years.

I was surprised at how comfortable I had gotten with David so quickly. I had really only known him for a little over two weeks. I guess spending time with him twenty-four hours a day made me familiar with him pretty quickly. I was enjoying getting to know him and getting to know about his life. He also seemed to know more about mine than I did.

David had a really great personality and I found him easy to talk to. That, and he was incredibly attractive. He had an adorable smile, and as we talked, he smiled at me whenever he looked over at me. It just seemed a natural reaction to smile back at him.

A few hours later, we stopped for lunch. It was fast food, but I was okay with a burger and fries. When we got back in the car, I decided to start reading David's journal. I had put it off because I was enjoying my conversation with David. However, I needed to know what my father had told him. I needed to see if I could find any more answers. I picked up the journal and continued reading where I had left off.

Journal Entry June 12, 2018

Arthur believes that Aurora is still alive because they wanted her alive. They had tried to abduct her from the hospital right after she was born. Luckily, that plan had been thwarted. They had also attempted to abduct her from a playground once when she was out with her nanny, but the security guards hired to protect her when Aurora went out with Annie stopped them.

There was another time when Abigail had taken Aurora with her to the community center. A homeless man had approached Aurora, and Abigail kept a close eye on them as they talked. A few minutes later, a man approached Abigail and began a conversation about the center and distracted her. When she looked back to where Aurora had been, both Aurora and the man she had been talking to were gone.

Abigail panicked, but then one of her security guards walked into the room carrying Aurora who was in tears. He led the homeless man in handcuffs in front of him. Later it was discovered that someone had paid the homeless man $100 and promised him another $100 if he got the little girl outside. He never got the man's name and the description he gave was vague at best.

Arthur wanted to keep Aurora locked in the house all day, but Abigail wanted her to have as close to a normal life as possible. It was not until both Abigail and Aurora were forced into a car by Abigail's father and brother that Abigail realized maybe Arthur was right. At least, until Aurora was older and could understand the dangers around her, she would be safer in the house.

Arthur had a security system installed in the house and made sure there was an armed guard at the house at all times. Abigail continued to take two security guards with her wherever she went. Annie agreed to stay in the house with Aurora. That would be all the normalcy she would know for a while.

Journal Entry June 19, 2018

The day that Abigail took Aurora with her to the salon, she did not take a security guard. Usually, she parked right in front of the salon, and the salon was always full of people. On this particular day, there were no close parking spots. Arthur believes that someone was watching everything they did and somehow knew that Abigail had an appointment that day.

Arthur also believes they filled the parking spots in front of the building so Abigail would have to walk. When they came out of the salon, it was easy to get a woman and child into a car. Abigail had told Arthur all about what happened in the car. Her father had only seemed interested in Aurora. He only spoke to Aurora until the little girl got out of the car. Then Victor spoke to Abigail.

Abigail told Arthur that Victor demanded they turn over Aurora to him before Aurora started school in the fall. Victor had already lost one daughter and Abigail was dead to him. He deserved another. The consequences would be severe if she did not comply. Abigail had cried when she told Arthur how scared she had been. He could have taken Aurora then, and she did not know why he did not. Victor had let them both go.

The only thing that made sense was how afraid Aurora had been of both Victor and Jimmy. Jimmy had pulled a gun on them, and Aurora had been terrified. If Victor genuinely thought that Arthur and Abigail would hand over their child to him, he must have believed they would prepare Aurora for this transition.

I looked up from reading and turned to look at David. "Did Victor really think a parent would just hand their kid over?" I asked him. He shrugged his shoulders.

"Victor is the kind of man that is used to getting what he wants. With your mother, I think she was the first to ever defy him when she married your father. He may have thought the threat was enough to convince them," he replied.

"Your mother would have known exactly what her father was capable of. That is probably why she agreed to keep you locked in the house," David continued. That did make sense. I just found it difficult to believe that no one had been arrested except a homeless man in all the attempts to abduct me.

"At the carnival, they weren't trying to kill me, were they?" I asked, realizing that they had murdered my mother because she married my father. The carnival had been another abduction attempt. They had almost gotten away with it too. They had gotten away with killing three people and framing my father for murder. If he had been there, he may have been killed as well. Then another thought entered my mind.

"So, why do they want me now? They can't expect that I'll come to them quietly. They sent goons after me to try and abduct me again, but they killed my mother and put my father in prison. That doesn't exactly endear them to me. I'm not calling that man Grandpa," I said.

"Well, maybe they found out that you had no memory somehow. They have no idea that you have started to remember, and they definitely have no idea that you are reading your father's interviews with me. Maybe they just think you will be happy to find your long-lost family," David replied.

I thought about that for a few minutes. "But sending two men to abduct me from my job doesn't really endear them to me either," I said. We both fell silent, content to ponder our own thoughts for a while. I wondered what they wanted with me now. As a five-year-old child, I could see them wanting to raise me and corrupt me from a young age. But I am twenty-four now. I have already been raised.

It could not be just about family either. My grandfather had said my mother was dead to him. Then he had her killed. Why didn't he just abduct her and bring her home? Maybe it was because she was already in the spotlight with my father. It was easier to kill my mother, frame my father, and abduct me and start over with a new child.

I was tired of thinking about all of it. I could feel the start of a headache, and I closed my eyes and leaned my head against the back of the seat. Suddenly, I felt David's hand on mine. I quickly opened my eyes and looked at him. "We are going to figure this out, okay?" he said. All I could do was nod.

How in the world were we going to figure this out? There was no evidence. My grandfather was currently looking for me to abduct me. I could not go home. David and I were basically on the run, and my father had been in prison for nineteen years for something he did not even do. One thing I did know, I had David with me. He was determined to find out the truth and that gave me hope.

I glanced over at him and he turned and gave me that adorable smile. My lips responded immediately with a smile. We would figure this out together. I looked down at his hand still on mine and I laced our fingers together. Then I closed my eyes once more.

Chapter 8

Just outside of Denver, we stopped for dinner. It
was a little hole-in-the-wall place, and it kind of reminded
me of the café I had worked at back in Salina. David and I
slid into the worn booth benches. A waitress arrived at
our table a few minutes later with menus. As I perused the
menu, I thought of something.

"David, we haven't talked about money. How
long can you afford for us to stay in Denver?" I asked
him. I saw a slow smile form on his lips. "Well, I am
actually on assignment, so I am being paid to be here," he
told me. My eyes opened wide in surprise.

"What's the story?" I asked him. "Well, it's some
disgruntled residents who are not excited for a new resort
that's supposed to be coming to their town. I will
interview the residents of the town and then some people
from the company that is wanting to build the resort. I
will supply both sides to my readers. I don't generally
take sides on an issue such as this one. I just like to report
on the facts," he replied.

That actually surprised me because I knew the media loved to influence viewers. It worked with my parents when my father was accused of having an affair. An honest reporter. For some reason, those words seemed contradictory. However, I had already come to trust David, so he must be made of a different cloth.

Deciding to let him worry about the money since he had dragged me all the way to Colorado, I gave my order to the waitress. The food was actually really good here, especially considering the inexpensive prices. Of course, I was not a very picky eater. Just feed me when I am hungry, and I am good.

When we got to Denver, David stayed on the interstate. I did not ask him where we were headed, figuring I would find out soon enough. It did not really matter. Until we came up with some kind of plan, we did not have much to do. We drove for another hour and were in a small town about thirty minutes outside of Denver. David pulled into a motel parking lot and parked the car. "I'll be right back," he said, getting out and locking the doors behind him.

I waited for about fifteen minutes, wondering what we were doing here. Finally, David walked out to the car. He pulled the car over in front of one of the rooms and got out. "Come on," he said. "We are number eight." I looked up in surprise at the door in front of us with a plastic number eight screwed into it.

I slowly opened the car door and got out, looking at the door in front of us. David was grabbing our bags out of the trunk. When he slammed the trunk shut, I still had not moved. David walked to the door and put a key in the knob and opened it. Then he turned back to look at me.

"Come on," he said again, and walked inside. I took a deep breath and closed the car door, then walked towards the motel room door that David had just gone through. When I opened it and looked around, it looked like any other motel room, not that I had seen a lot. There were two double beds, a dresser with a tv on it, a bedside table between the two beds, and a table with two chairs under it against the window to my left. On the floor next to the dresser was a mini fridge.

I stepped inside the room and let the door close behind me. David looked over at me. "You want the bed by the window or the one by the bathroom?" he asked me. What he said had not yet registered as I was still looking around the room and thinking about sharing the room with David. Before I knew he had moved, David stepped in front of me and lifted my hands. The contact jolted me, and I looked up at him.

"Aurora, you already know I would never hurt you. I would have gotten two rooms, but we don't know how long we will be here. I don't want the money to run out too soon," he said softly. I nodded then looked back to the beds. "By the bathroom," I said quietly.

He let my hands fall and picked up my bag and put it on the bed closer to the bathroom. His bag he tossed on the other bed. Then he sat down on the bed he would be using. He looked up at me where I still stood just inside the door. "Aurora, come sit," he said softly, pointing at the other bed.

I sighed deeply then made myself walk across the room to the other bed. I sat down, testing the mattress that I would be sleeping on for who knows how long. I looked down at the floor feeling extremely uncomfortable. "I've never shared a room before," I finally admitted, not able to look David in the eye.

"Well, I am a pretty heavy sleeper, so if you snore, it won't wake me up," David said, and I looked up to see the grin on his face. My mouth responded automatically with a smile. "Look, I will consider that bed your personal space and this bed my personal space. We have a table for meals or paperwork. But we may have to fight for the remote control," he said, and I felt my smile grow bigger. He was trying to make me comfortable.

"Do you sleep with the tv on or off?" he asked me next. I thought about that for a minute. I did not usually sleep with a tv on, but I knew I would not sleep if it was too quiet either. "Well, I have to have some kind of noise. I can't sleep when it is totally quiet," I told him. "I am the same way," he replied. "We will try turning it down low when we go to bed."

I headed to the shower first, but I was too self-conscious to sleep without a bra on. When I was fully dressed, I exited the bathroom. David headed to the shower next. Sharing a bathroom would be interesting as well. I flipped through the tv channels but there really was not anything on to watch.

David walked out of the bathroom in only a pair of shorts. I tried not to notice his abs or biceps or the hair on his chest, but it was difficult not to notice how toned he was. I managed to draw my eyes away from him and back to the tv. This was going to be a long…well, however many days this was going to take.

"Are you ready for sleep?" David asked me as he sat down on his bed. I definitely did not think I could handle a face-to-face conversation with him right now, so I just nodded and pulled the covers down. I laid down and pulled the covers up over me. I turned just enough to toss the tv remote to David, then looked up and stared at the ceiling.

We currently had no plan. We had no evidence. We were sitting in a motel room outside of Denver, and the only person I knew here was in a prison an hour away. Well, that and the half-naked man in the bed next to mine. I rolled over and turned my back to David. This was going to be a long night.

I woke to a thin stream of light coming through a slit in the curtains. Sitting up, I looked over at the other bed. It was empty. I swallowed down a moment of panic as I got out of bed and headed to the bathroom. Once I brushed my teeth, I walked back into the room and went to the window. Pulling back the curtain, I saw that David's car was gone. I guess all I could do now was wait for him to return.

I picked up the tv remote from the table between the beds and sat down on my bed. Flipping through the channels, I did not really pay attention to what was on. It was just something to do and kept my hands busy. A few minutes later, I heard a key in the door and David walked in.

"Good morning," he said with a smile. "I've got breakfast." He held up a bag. When we were both seated at the table with our food, I looked up at him. "What's the plan?" I asked him. "Well, I need to go speak with your father," he said in a serious tone. I knew he would never agree to let me go with him, so I did not even ask.

"And I just get to sit here in the room," I said instead, somewhat dejectedly. "You have some journals to read," he reminded me. At least that would give me something to do. David left about thirty minutes later, and I sat down on the bed with the stack of journals and started to read once more.

Journal Entry June 26, 2018

Arthur told me that he was supposed to be going to the carnival with Abigail and Aurora that fateful evening. Just before they were to leave the house, Arthur got a phone call. That call changed everything for all of them. If he had not taken that call, he might have ended up dead as well. Aurora had been pretty upset that Arthur would not be going with them, so he promised he would come when he was done on the phone.

As he was driving to the carnival over an hour later, he saw Aurora in his headlights tumbling down the steep dirt cliff at the side of the road. When he stopped the car and ran to her, all she said was, "Mommy is dead." Then she collapsed in his arms. He quickly put her in the car and turned the car around, knowing that he had to keep Aurora safe.

He drove straight out of Colorado that night and took Aurora somewhere that no one would find her. He has not yet told me where she is, and I wonder how far he took her. When he returned the next day, the police were waiting for him and he was arrested. Someone had seen his car on the road that night, and it looked as if he was leaving the carnival in a hurry. He never admitted to being at the carnival and he told the police he did not know where his daughter was.

The same woman who had claimed to be having an affair came forward as a witness during the trial. Elizabeth Harvey. She claimed that Arthur had said he was going to get rid of his wife and child so they could be together. When questioned further, she told the jury that she thought he just meant he was going to divorce Abigail.

I stopped reading there. Elizabeth Harvey. We had to find her. She might have some answers. She had tried twice to discredit my father, and the second time put him in prison. It was at least a place to start. I wondered what was happening with David and my father but knew I would just have to be patient and wait for him to return.

Chapter 9

I read through to the end of the first journal and had picked up the second one when the door opened. I swung my legs over the side of the bed and looked up at David expectantly. He sat down on the bed across from me, and I waited anxiously for him to speak. "Your father is fine. He said to tell you that he loves you," David said gently. It took me a few moments to respond as I tried to get control of my emotions.

"Did he give you any clue what we are supposed to do now?" I asked him. "He is not sure. Now that they know for sure that you are alive, it is even more important that you stay hidden," he told me. I could feel my body heating up as my anger started to build. I jumped up from the bed and glared at him.

"You can't just lock me away in this motel room. It may have worked when I was five, but not now. I am going to help you with this and if you don't like that, I will just leave. You can't keep me as a prisoner," I replied. David looked at me in surprise. Somehow, he had managed to remain calm after my outburst.

"And just where do you think you will go?" he asked me quietly. "To see Elizabeth Harvey," I told him, my eyes not leaving his. I did not raise my voice this time, and I watched David as he watched me. I could tell he was thinking. It was a few minutes before he finally spoke.

"I haven't read through those journals in quite a while, and I am not sure why that didn't come to me sooner. That may just be a perfect place to start," he said, surprising me. He pulled out his laptop and sat down at the table. Sitting down on the edge of my bed once again, I watched him and waited patiently for him to search for Elizabeth.

With David being a reporter, it took a lot longer than I expected. He explained it was because she had gotten married, then divorced, then married again and had moved around quite a lot. Finally, he had managed to locate her. She no longer lived in Denver, but it was only a thirty-minute drive to where she currently lived. David and I both headed to the car.

Thirty minutes later, David and I both wondered if we had the right address. We pulled in front of a run-down mobile home in the middle of a neighborhood of run-down mobile homes. I looked over at David as he reached beneath his seat and pulled out a gun. He must have seen the shocked expression on my face. "As a reporter, I go to a lot of, let's just say, not very nice places. You can never be too safe," he explained. He tucked the gun in his waistband and pulled his shirt down over it.

We both stepped out of the car and approached the door of the mobile home in front of us. I had no idea what Elizabeth even looked like, but when the door opened a few moments after we knocked, David seemed to recognize the woman standing in the doorway. She looked as if she had been beautiful once, and she had aged well.

"Elizabeth, hi, my name is David, and this is Aurora," David said. At the mention of my name, Elizabeth quickly looked over at me. She studied my face for a few moments, then looked back at David. "What do you want?" she asked in a defensive tone. "We just want to talk with you for a few minutes," David said softly. I did not think she was going to agree as she just stared at me for a few more moments. Finally, she stepped back and motioned us into her home.

The inside of her home was just as run-down as the outside. I was not sure what to do so I just followed David. He walked inside and sat down on the couch and gave Elizabeth a smile. She sat down on a chair across from us and looked over at me. What she said next startled me.

"You look just like your mother," she said softly, her eyes never leaving mine. David spoke next. "Why did you do it?" he asked her. That question held a lot of questions. We wanted to know why she claimed to be having a relationship with my father. Why did she testify falsely against him at his trial, and what did she have to gain from it?

I watched as her gaze went to David, then she looked down at the floor. I wondered if she would answer and I wondered if she would give us the answers we needed. We did not have to wait long. "I was an escort. I worked for Jimmy at one of his casinos. He told me if I helped him with this, he would set me up so that I didn't have to be an escort anymore. What girl wouldn't want to get away from that life?" she asked, looking up at us. Her eyes were full of sorrow, and she sighed heavily before continuing.

"Jimmy told me that I would be done with that life. When the trial was over, he set me up in a nice little house and found me a decent job. I thought that the old life was over. I found a good man and we got married. He didn't know anything about my past. Two years later, Jimmy showed up. He wanted me to do another job. He wanted me to keep a man occupied for the night. He was going to give us a hotel room at a ritzy place, but I just couldn't do it," she explained, looking down at the floor once again.

"I loved my husband, and I couldn't go through with it. Jimmy told my husband about my past and that I had been an escort and had worked for him. My husband left me. Jimmy ruined my life. It's what I deserved for ruining yours," she said quietly, and my eyes opened wide. I glanced over at David.

"There is a way to fix this," he said gently to her. "There is an innocent man in prison right now because of you. You are the only one that can make this right," he told her. She looked at David, over to me, and back to David. Then she shook her head. I quickly stood to my feet.

"What do you mean by that? You are the only one who can fix this," I said, my voice raised, and my fists balled at my side. David grabbed ahold of my arm and pulled me back down to the couch beside him. He gave me a look that said, "Shut up now." I looked over at Elizabeth. "You don't understand. Jimmy will kill me," Elizabeth said, and I could see the look of fear on her face.

"What about the man that Jimmy wanted you to distract. Do you know who that was? Do you know his name? Or why you were supposed to keep him busy?" David asked. Elizabeth nodded. "It was Evan Arnold. He owned another casino and was competition for Jimmy. Jimmy wanted something out of Evan's office. I was supposed to keep him busy all night so they would have plenty of time to find whatever it was," she told us.

David stood and took my hand, pulling me from the couch. "Thank you, Elizabeth. You have been extremely helpful. Please, do not worry. We will not tell anyone that we spoke with you or that we were here," he told her. Then he pulled me towards the door. I wondered how in the world she had been helpful. She had refused to help us.

Chapter 10

When we got to the car, neither of us spoke. David turned out of Elizabeth's neighborhood and all I could do was sit and stare at him. He had to have some kind of plan, but I knew he would not tell me anything until he was ready. "For someone as patient as you are, I'm kind of surprised that you lost your cool back there," he finally said. I looked at him with a shocked expression and he laughed.

"I have never met anyone as patient as you. I would have thought you would have bombarded me with questions the moment we got in the car. I have been waiting for it actually," he told me. I felt myself sigh. "I learned from my grandparents that I can ask five hundred questions, but if they did not want to give me the information, I was just wasting my breath. I figured if you wanted me to know what you are thinking, you would tell me. Harassing you about it may just annoy you and then you might not tell me anything," I replied honestly. He gave me a funny look.

"Go ahead. Ask," he said. "Okay, how exactly was she helpful?" I asked him. "Well, I knew that she was not going to help us in the way we wanted her to, and there is nothing we can do about that. She is the kind of person that if she got backed into a corner, she would run. You saw her place. She would not be leaving anything important behind if she decided to skip town," he explained.

"Okay, I get that. I mean, I could see how she would be scared of my mother's family. But how exactly did she help us?" I asked again. "The information she gave us is what we are going to look into. Evan Arnold. Does that name sound familiar to you at all?" he asked me, and I shook my head.

"Should it?" I asked him in reply. "Well, he made the headlines back in 2009. It was all over the news. I wasn't a journalist yet, but I was in college and a lot of my classes used current events. He was arrested for money laundering. He was not found guilty on that charge, but several of his employees were. He went to prison for a few years on lesser charges. He ran a casino that was in competition with your uncle's, as Elizabeth told us," he said.

I thought about this for a few moments. "You think my uncle is the reason he got caught?" I asked him, and he nodded. "I happen to know that he lives not too far from here," he told me. I was impressed. David obviously knew what he was doing. I seemed to be just along for the ride. That, and my uncle or grandfather were trying to find me. At least David did not leave me in the hotel room.

We drove into a quiet neighborhood with small but nice houses along both sides. When David pulled into the driveway of a small white house with dark green shutters, I wondered what we would find. I glanced at David hesitantly, but he just smiled at me and got out. I followed him.

The door opened just a moment after David knocked. A portly older gentleman stood in front of us. "May I help you?" he asked us, looking from one of us to the other. I looked at David knowing he would handle this. Mr. Arnold was not familiar to me at all.

"Mr. Arnold, may we come in and speak with you? We have some information that will be worth your time," David said. "Who are you?" Mr. Arnold asked. "My name is David," he said, then paused and looked at me. "This is Aurora Davis," he continued. I saw the surprise on Mr. Arnold's face as he studied me closely.

"You look just like your mother," he finally said softly. "May we come in?" David asked again. This time, Mr. Arnold opened the door wide and pointed towards the couch in the small living room. The three of us sat down and Mr. Arnold openly stared at me from the armchair across from us. I was beginning to feel uncomfortable.

"We all thought you were dead," he said quietly. "No, I am very much alive, and my father did not kill my mother," I replied. Mr. Arnold nodded. "I did not believe that he had. Your father was an incredibly good man. His only fault was marrying Victor Smaldone's daughter," he told us. "What information is it that you say I will want to hear?" he asked, looking at David.

"Mr. Arnold, when you were arrested, I am assuming that some evidence showed up that had been locked away, maybe in a safe in your office?" David asked. Mr. Arnold's face registered surprise. "Yes. To this day, I don't know how the FBI got it. I was the only one that knew what was in there, and I was the only one with the combination to that safe," he told us.

"We know how they got it," David said, and Mr. Arnold's jaw dropped open. David told him about our visit with Elizabeth, but he did not mention her name. He explained how Jimmy had tried to coerce her into keeping him occupied all night while Jimmy, or some of Jimmy's people, searched Mr. Arnold's office. Mr. Arnold's face went pale as he listened to David speak.

When David had finished, Mr. Arnold stood from the sofa and began to pace the small living room. There was only enough room for four steps in one direction and four steps back. "That happened. Just like you said. Obviously, they found another girl to manipulate. It was just two days later that I was arrested," he told us as he continued to pace, looking down at the floor. When he stopped, he looked over at us.

"What is it you want from me? I am sure you did not just come here to tell me this," he asked next. "We need your help," David said. "We figured you would be interested in taking the Smaldones down, and we need to get Arthur out of prison. He has been there for nineteen years for a crime he didn't commit," David explained.

Mr. Arnold sat down again, and we spent the next two hours discussing how to get my father out of prison. Mr. Arnold knew quite a lot about Jimmy's casinos and some of the corruption he had been involved in. They had even worked together a few times to get rid of a common threat. However, we had to get some kind of evidence. We needed a plan. We needed to find some way to take Jimmy down, and Mr. Arnold was very willing to help. He told us that he still had a lot of connections.

He told us that my grandfather had gotten out of politics, and no one had seen or heard from him in several years. Victor would be in his seventies now and was probably retired somewhere. He was probably living like a king while my father sat in prison for a crime that Victor or Jimmy was responsible for. Maybe we should just go to the police.

I let the men talk while I sat quietly, lost in my own thoughts. Maybe I could find an attorney that would be willing to help my dad. Maybe I could go to the FBI.

They had gotten involved in arresting Mr. Arnold, but that was because his business had crossed state lines.

Then my thoughts went to the house I had lived in. I pictured my mom and dad dressed for the gala. Then I could see the white marble floors and the two large columns that were built into the wall. Suddenly, I realized that was where I had hidden. The column had swung open, and Annie had shoved me inside and shut it.

I could picture my father's office with the dark wooden paneling and built-in bookshelves. When my parents were not home, sometimes I would hide under his desk when Annie and I played hide-and-seek. The dining room had a long table, and I could picture myself, along with my mother and father, sitting at the table eating dinner. I had a wooden booster on the seat of the chair that I sat on.

I could remember running up the wide staircase and opening the door to my sitting room. Annie and I ate a lot of meals in there together. The table we ate at was against one of the two windows and I used to look out the window while I ate. My bed I had always thought was huge, but I had been only five. I remembered that Annie had lain beside me many times when I was too scared to go to sleep alone.

I did not realize that tears were rolling down my cheeks until I felt David's fingers on my face. I looked up at him as he wiped the tears away. "I remember," I whispered. He laced his fingers through mine and I was comforted by that small gesture. I leaned against his shoulder.

When we were in the car and headed back to the motel, David looked over at me. "What did you remember?" he asked me. "Everything," I told him honestly. "Well, everything that an almost six-year-old would remember. I can picture our house, my father's office, my bedroom, eating dinner with my parents. I remember more about Annie because my parents were gone a lot," I explained.

"I remember hiding in the column across from the staircase the night Annie was shot. The column on the right opened up and she shoved me inside. I can still hear my grandfather's voice. He was definitely there. I don't know if he was the one that actually shot Annie, but he was definitely there looking for me," I told him.

David was quiet for a few minutes and I wondered what he was thinking. "There's something I have not told you," he finally said, and I watched him carefully. "Your house, the house you lived in, Jimmy lives there now. He got it pretty cheap after your father's conviction," he told me, and my mouth dropped open in shock. My fists balled as I felt my initial shock replaced with anger.

They killed Annie, killed my mother, framed my father, changed my whole life, and then moved into our home. I could not speak as the anger boiled inside of me. I had never felt such rage. It consumed me and I struggled to breathe. Neither of us spoke until we pulled in front of our motel room. David got out of the car, but I did not move.

I felt, more than heard, my car door open, and David reached in and unbuckled my seatbelt. He took my hand firmly, but gently, and pulled me out of the car. When I was standing in front of him, his other hand gently moved my chin until I was looking up at him.

"We will get them. We will make them pay for what they have done," he told me softly, and I could see the sincerity of his words in his eyes. "They are not going to get away with this. I told you I would find answers, and I am not going to stop looking until we have them," he continued.

I just nodded at him, unable to speak. He pulled me against his chest and wrapped his arms around me. There were no tears, but I clung to him. I was afraid. Afraid we would not find any answers and afraid my uncle would find me. I was afraid that I might never see my father again. David kept his arm around me as we walked into our room.

Chapter 11

I must have been exhausted because I fell asleep quickly that night and woke up early in the morning. There was only a soft light coming in through the crack between the curtains, and I looked over and saw that David was still asleep. When I went to sleep, he had been sitting on his bed with his laptop open in his lap and I had no idea when he had finally gone to bed.

I was surprised that I had not dreamed last night. That was very unusual for me, but I was grateful that I had not had a nightmare. Lying in bed, I thought about the memories I now had that had never been there before. When I saw David move, I looked over at him and saw his eyes were open and he was watching me. I could not help smiling at him.

"Good morning," he said. I felt the heat rise in my cheeks. This should have been very awkward, waking up looking at a man beside me, but for some reason it was not. I turned to face him, my head still on the pillow. "What is our plan today?" I asked him.

"Well, since I am officially here for work, I have to actually do some work. Do you want to take a ride with me and see what a reporter does?" he asked with a grin. "I am pretty sure I saw that yesterday, but there is no way you are leaving me here in this room," I told him. He just laughed.

When we were dressed and back in the car, he pulled into a drive-thru for some breakfast. Then we were on the road again. He explained a little about the small town we were going to visit. It was about a thirty-minute drive from the town to the nearest ski resort and was a central location for another resort to be built. However, the community did not want another resort. They liked their small town just the way it was, and currently, they already received visits from tourists that spilled over from the ski resorts around them.

What the locals did not know was that the property had already been purchased and the resort was coming, like it or not. David had an inside source that had confirmed this information to him, but it was not yet common knowledge. "Well, you don't have to worry about me telling anyone," I told him, and he laughed.

When we arrived at the town, David drove up and down the streets so we could look around. Their Main Street was like something out of an old western. The shops were all connected down both sides of the street. Some of the fronts of the shops had been covered in brick, and some wore fresh paint, but the buildings looked incredibly old. The shop signs were made to look like they were from the Wild West.

The street and shops were all so charming, and people strolled up and down the sidewalks. At the end of Main Street was a large park. The road curved around the park like an enormous roundabout. There were picnic tables, park benches, and several large playground sets. With the mountains as a backdrop, it was straight out of a painting. I could see why the residents did not want a change.

We drove around the park and David headed us back towards Main Street. He found a parking spot, and we walked towards the closest shop. Once we stepped inside, I browsed the aisles of merchandise while David headed to the counter to see if he could speak with the owner of the shop.

I heard him introduce himself as a reporter and he told the man why he was here. The man was very eager to answer any and all of David's questions. This turned out to be the same in the next five shops we entered. Once they found out that David was a reporter and was asking about how the residents felt about the resort coming to their small town, everyone wanted to talk.

David stopped a few people on the sidewalk, and after finding out if they were locals, he asked them questions as well. We strolled Main Street for about two hours with David stopping random people or stepping into different types of shops. I noticed that along with the shop owners, he spoke with people from all different age groups.

The next place we walked into was a sandwich shop. David held the door as I stepped inside. I was prepared to wait by the door, but David put his hand on the small of my back and led me forward. "You hungry?" he asked me. My stomach replied for me by rumbling loudly and David and I both laughed. "I'll take that as a yes," he said, grinning at me.

We got our food and sat down at a table. We talked about the town and what we had seen of it so far. I realized that I was beginning to feel a little homesick. This place was beautiful, but I missed my Kansas prairie. It was odd to remember that I had once lived very close to here. I did not remember much about Denver, and Salina was definitely where I considered my home.

When we were finished eating, we drove away from downtown and into a neighborhood. I told David that I would stay in the car while he knocked on a few doors and spoke with the residents. Soon we were back on the road and headed back to the motel. I was lost in my own thoughts all the way.

I had missed a lot of the conversation between David and Mr. Arnold, but David said that Mr. Arnold still had a lot of contacts in the casino world. He was going to see what he could find out about Jimmy's current financial condition and any rumors that might be going around. When he heard something, he would contact David. For now, we really had nothing to do but wait.

When we got back to our room, I sat down on the edge of my bed. Frustration is what I was currently feeling. David sat down on his bed across from me. "What are you thinking?" he asked me softly. I looked over at him. "How frustrating this whole situation is," I replied honestly.

"Can't we go to the police or an attorney? With what I remember, I can prove that Victor was in my house the night that Annie was killed. I can remember the two men that killed my mother and chased me at the carnival. I did not recognize them, but it obviously was not my father," I said, hearing the frustration in my voice and knowing that David could too.

"We could, but we don't have anything on Jimmy. You won't be safe until we can put Jimmy away. Victor isn't running the show anymore, and it's even possible that he is already dead. The only thing going to the police would do is make you a target. Even if your dad got out of prison, he would also become a target. He is safe where he is, and Jimmy will leave him alone while he is there," David explained.

"A target," I said, running ideas through my head. "What if I become bait. If Jimmy wants me that bad, why don't we catch him trying to take me. If we went to the police, I could wear a wire. They could catch him in the act," I said, already knowing that I was grasping at straws and that David would never agree with this plan. The look he gave me said it all, and I felt myself sigh in frustration.

"We have no way of even knowing that the police would believe us. Believe you. You were only five years old when it happened. Not to mention, if Jimmy wants you dead, he may just shoot you. I am not letting you put yourself in unnecessary danger," he replied. I was quick with my response.

"If he wanted me dead, he would have had those men at the café kill me instead of follow me around for two weeks. He obviously wants me alive for some reason," I told him. But David had also been considering the whole situation. He was just as quick with his own reply back to me.

"He may just want to know what you know or what you remember. If he finds a wire on you, he might just kill you. If he finds out that you don't know anything, he might kill you. If he finds out what you do know, he may decide he got what he wanted and doesn't need you anymore and then kill you. When he finds out that you don't want to become part of his happy little family, he might kill you," he said.

"Okay, okay. I get it," I replied. "I'm just tired of waiting. There doesn't seem to be an end in sight," I continued, looking down at my hands in my lap. David leaned forward and wrapped his hands around mine. The beds were close enough together if we both moved to the very edge of the bed, our knees would touch.

"I know your memories have just come back, and that has to be overwhelming. I know you are frustrated, and believe me, I am just as frustrated. But we can't just go storming in there and demanding answers from Jimmy. He is a pro at using people and getting to people, and he has a lot of unscrupulous people that work for him. I couldn't bear if something were to happen to you. I would blame myself. I need for you to be safe," he said gently.

I looked up at him and saw the sincerity on his face. I could tell he wanted to say more, so I waited. "Aurora, the first time I saw you, I wanted to approach you and talk to you, but I couldn't. All I could do was watch you from a distance. It was very frustrating as I looked into your life. You are beautiful and kind, and you always think of others."

"I told you once that I enjoy observing people and learning about human behavior. I was supposed to be watching you to make sure you were safe, but I learned so much more about you. You are one of the most fascinating people that I have met. At Elizabeth's house, that was the first time I have ever seen you lose control like that."

"You have better control of your emotions than anyone I have ever known. Your patience astounds me, and everything I learn about you just makes me want to know more. I know you have only known me for a short time, and I don't expect you to feel the same way about me. But I know you trust me, and that is enough for me right now. I would never hurt you, and I will protect you with my life," he told me honestly.

When he was done speaking, I did not know what to say. He was right. I did trust him completely. My father trusted him as well, and that said a lot. My father had chosen David to watch out for me, and David had done just that. I also knew that I felt safe with David around.

I stood from the bed and took a step towards David's bed and sat down next to him. He wrapped his arms around my shoulder, and I leaned against his chest with my arm around his back. My other hand was still in his. My next thought was what would happen between us when this was all over. I realized that was too far ahead to think about and I shifted my thoughts back to this moment and David.

I knew that David had opened himself up to me and had been completely honest just now. My thoughts became jumbled and my emotions were not something I even wanted to think about right now. I knew I felt safe, and I was not afraid. I knew that I had been afraid a lot when I was five and I remembered Annie laying in my bed beside me. Now I knew that was because of my uncle and grandfather.

"What are you thinking?" David asked me softly. It took me a few moments to answer. "I was thinking about how safe I feel right now. I remember as a child being afraid a lot. I have always had nightmares, and sometimes I was just afraid to go to sleep because I didn't want to dream. I didn't dream at all the last two nights, and that is very unusual for me," I told him.

I looked up at him. "I can only assume that is because I knew you were here," I continued. His gaze was intense as he looked down at me. He really was very handsome, and I found myself wanting him to kiss me. It surprised me when he closed his eyes and turned his head away from me. "What are you thinking?" I asked him in return. He turned back to look at me.

"Well, honestly, I was thinking about how much I would really like to kiss you right now, but I can't. We have to get through this together, and that needs to be our focus. That, and I am afraid that if I kissed you, I wouldn't be able to stop," he replied softly. I laid my head back against his chest and felt his arm tighten around me. We sat like that for a few more minutes, neither of us talking, but both of us thinking about the other.

Chapter 12

About an hour later, David went to find a grocery store. We were limited with the types of food we could fix in the room, but salad, sandwiches, some fresh fruit, and cereal for breakfast was fine with me. David also got packages of paper plates, paper bowls, and plastic silverware.

That night, when we both got into bed, we turned and faced each other. We talked about our lives growing up. I did not know anything about David's life, and he knew nothing of mine after I left Colorado until he started watching me. Other than being raised by an older couple, we found that he and I had been raised remarkably similar.

Our families celebrated holidays the same way and fixed a lot of the same types of food. We discussed our favorites meals and foods we did not like. Our schools had been similar in size, and he had also lived outside of town. We had been disciplined the same way as children, but he got into a lot more trouble than I did. He and I also had similar views on politics, and we discussed some of the current things that were happening in the political world. He did not have any brothers or sisters, so we talked about how we had spent our time growing up.

I did not remember falling asleep, and when I woke up, I was quite sure that I had fallen asleep in the middle of David talking. I looked over at him still sleeping and smiled at the thought. He had become a friend, and even more than that. I had never had anyone to talk to like he and I did last night.

I watched him sleeping for quite some time before I decided to get up and head to the bathroom for a shower. When I got out of the bed, I looked over at him and saw his eyes open. "Good morning," I said quietly, smiling down at him. "Good morning," he replied with a smile.

"I apologize if I fell asleep while you were talking," I told him, and he chuckled. "I could tell when you were close to falling asleep. That's why I didn't ask you anymore questions," he admitted, and I laughed. "Well, I slept really well. So, thank you for that. No dreams last night either," I said.

"Well, good. Maybe that will become the new normal for you," he said sincerely. I really hoped that was true. When I finished in the bathroom, David headed to the shower. I fixed a bowl of cereal and sat down at the table to eat. When David finished and stepped out of the bathroom, his cellphone rang. He walked over to where it lay on the table beside the bed. "It's Evan Arnold," he told me and answered the call.

They talked for about fifteen minutes. When David hung up the call, he turned and looked at me with a serious expression. I waited, knowing he would tell me when he was ready. "Come here," he said gently, and I could not read the look in his eyes. I stood from the chair and walked around his bed to where he stood between the two beds.

He opened his arms and I did not hesitate to step into them. I wrapped my arms around his waist and laid my head against his chest. His arms came around me and held me tightly. "Aurora, I need for you to stay here," he said softly. I tried to pull away, feeling the anger building inside of me, but his arms held me tightly against him. I dropped my forehead to his chest and stopped struggling. There was no point.

"Will you at least tell me why?" I asked him. "I am going to be meeting with some not particularly good people. People that Mr. Arnold worked with in the past. I don't want them to know that you are here because I don't trust them. Mr. Arnold says they have information that we need, and I believe him, but I don't know these people. I need to know that you will be safe," he replied.

I nodded my head against his chest so that he would know I agreed to stay. I did not trust my voice to speak, so I just held onto him. "And what if you don't come back?" I finally asked him, afraid that this was a possibility. He took me by the shoulders and pushed me back until I could see his face. His expression was serious.

"Aurora, I will be back. I promise you that," he said, but I knew that was a promise he should not have made. No one knows what the future holds. "I'm holding you to that promise. Don't let me down," I replied softly. He kissed the top of my head then dropped his hands and grabbed his keys. I closed my eyes as he walked out the door.

I sat down on my bed and looked at the door, staring at it for a long time after he left. David had given me no idea of how long he would be gone, and my mind started running through what all could happen to him. If something did happen to him, I did not know what I would do. How would I even know? I did not have a cell phone, and I would be stranded in a motel with no transportation and no money. There was no one here in Colorado that I knew except for the people who were searching for me.

Reaching over to the table beside the bed, I picked up the remote to the tv. The room was far too quiet, and I needed a distraction from my thoughts. Worry was not a friend of mine although it seems to have found me a lot lately. I flipped through the channels and finally stopped on a movie I had seen before. Nothing else was on but news and sports.

When that movie was over, another one came on and I watched it. Around 1:00 in the afternoon, I made a sandwich for lunch and ate an apple. Then I returned to my spot on the bed and watched another movie. Never in my life had I watched so much tv or sat still for so long.

At 4:00 in the afternoon, I began pacing the small room. All I could think about was what if something had happened to David. By 11:00 that night, he had still not returned. I crawled under the covers and turned the volume on the tv down so that I could just hear what the actors were saying.

Maybe the people he was meeting with had to wait until nighttime to get the information. I wondered if David was participating in something illegal. That worried me, along with already worrying if he was okay. I glanced at the clock on the table beside the bed and saw that it was 12:03. I could not keep my eyes open any longer.

I was at the carnival with my mother. Everything around me was familiar. The lights. The sounds. The crowds of people. I had been here before. I rode the tilt-a-whirl with my mother, but neither of us laughed or smiled. We were both apprehensive, as if we knew that something bad was going to happen.

When the ride was over, we got into the line to ride again. I glanced around, watching the people moving around us. I saw my Uncle Jimmy standing in the line of another ride. He looked right at me and his look was menacing. I held on tighter to my mother's hand and looked up at her. I could see fear in her eyes.

When she pulled me from the line, we both ran. We headed towards the tree line. Suddenly, her hand dropped from mine. I kept running, but when I looked back at her, I saw both David and her lying on the ground. Blood pooled around them both and their eyes stared at nothing. I felt the scream in my throat as I turned and ran.

When I reached the tree line, I kept running. I could feel the branches scratching my hands and face and snagging on my clothes. The footsteps behind me got closer, and then I was falling. I screamed again as I felt hands on my shoulders, and I heard someone calling my name.

I opened my eyes and screamed again, afraid that the men had caught me. I struggled against the hands that held me. "Aurora, it's David. You are dreaming. Wake up!" I heard. My eyes cleared and I realized I was in the bed in our motel room. David sat on the bed beside me, his hands still on my shoulders and a look of concern on his face.

I sat up quickly and my arms went around his neck. I choked on a sob. "David. They killed you. They killed you and my mother," I cried. "Shhhh. I am okay. I am here and I'm safe," he said as I clung to him. When the dream had completely faded and my initial fear was over, I looked up at David.

"I'm sorry that I was gone so long," he said quietly. My arms were still around his neck and I was hesitant to let him go. "I was so afraid. Even before the dream," I whispered, not trusting my voice. He put his arms around me again and pulled me against him. "I'm sorry for worrying you," he replied.

We stayed like this for a few minutes. Finally, I leaned back and looked up at him. "When did you get back?" I asked him. "Only about twenty minutes ago," he answered. "I had just gotten in bed when you cried out," he continued. "Please don't leave me," I told him, hearing the panic in my voice. Then I moved over in the bed so he would know what I meant.

He grabbed a pillow from his bed and climbed into the bed beside me. "Do you want to talk about it?" he asked me when we were both laying down and facing each other. I closed my eyes and took a deep breath. "It was the same dream. It's always the same dream. I'm at the carnival. My mother and I ride the tilt-a-whirl. But then the dream changes. This time, I saw my Uncle Jimmy. He was standing in the line for another ride. And when they killed my mother, I saw you too. They killed you. There was so much blood and you were dead," I told him, choking on the sob in my throat.

His arms came around me and I buried my face in his chest. It was more than I could handle, and I cried. The tears would not stop, and I could not get the picture of his lifeless body out of my head. I felt his arms around me as I cried, and I held him as tightly as I could, afraid that this might be a dream and he was not really here.

"Aurora, I'm sorry," I heard him say softly. That halted my tears. I wiped the moisture from my face and looked up at him. "Don't apologize for coming back to me," I whispered, my eyes watching his. Then I closed my eyes. My head was laying on his shoulder, and my arm was around his waist. His other arm was around me and his hand was on my back. When I fell asleep, I did not dream the rest of the night.

Chapter 13

When I woke the next morning, my head was still on David's shoulder. He was lying on his back, and my arm was across his stomach. He was still asleep, and I could feel every inhale and exhale he made. I had not dreamed again once I knew he was safe. David had somehow become an emotional rabbit's foot for me, and I knew that I needed him.

I did not move and tried to keep my breathing steady so that I did not wake him. It was only 7:00 in the morning, and David had only gotten a few hours of sleep. I was content to just lie there, feeling him beside me. He was safe, and that was all that mattered.

I tried not to think about the fact that I was in bed with a man. He was asleep and I was awake, but this was new territory for me. I was wearing a t-shirt and shorts, but he only had on a pair of shorts. It was hard to resist running my hands through the hair on his chest, and I closed my eyes so I would not be tempted.

I must have fallen asleep again because I felt David move. He turned from his back to his side and his arm went around me in a possessive motion. It woke me up and I looked at him. His eyes were open, and our faces were only inches apart. He reached out and tucked a strand of my hair behind my ear.

"David," I whispered, and reached my hand up to his cheek. He smiled at me, then he kissed my forehead. He leaned his forehead against mine, and we stayed like this for several minutes. I closed my eyes and relished the closeness, overwhelmed again knowing that he was safe.

"Do you want to talk about the dream?" he asked softly. I leaned back and looked at him. "It's always the same dream. At the carnival. But bits and pieces change each time. I have never seen Jimmy there before. I used to see both my mother and father dead. This time it was you," I told him, fighting to hold back the tears that were threatening to fall. He held me tightly, my head tucked into his shoulder.

When he finally released me, I sat up and looked down at him. I did not move for several minutes as we watched each other. "Did you get enough sleep?" I finally asked him, and he nodded. "I'm going to go take a shower," I told him and stood from the bed. I did not trust myself to be in the bed with him any longer. I grabbed some clothes and realized we were going to have to do some laundry soon. It was a good thing the hotel had washers and dryers.

After my shower, David headed to the bathroom to take one. When he was done with his shower, we sat down at the table together with bowls of cereal for breakfast. "We found evidence against Jimmy," David said, startling me because I had been deep in thought. I looked up at him. "What did you find?" I asked him.

"Well, the escort service that Elizabeth told us about is actually a prostitution ring. One of the men I was with hired one of the women and recorded the transaction of money for sex. He didn't go through with it but paid her a lot of money to leave the hotel and come with him. Mr. Arnold has her hidden away until we can use her to testify against Jimmy," he told me.

"We know that he is involved in extortion and embezzlement, but we could not find any physical evidence of it. He probably keeps anything like that at his house," he continued. "My father's safe. It's in the wall behind his desk," I told him. Unfortunately, we had no way of getting to it.

"Is the evidence for prostitution enough to put him away?" I asked, and David nodded. "But it doesn't help your father," he replied. I realized this was true. Jimmy might go away, but my father would still be in prison. There really was no evidence of my father's innocence. If Elizabeth refused to testify and refute her previous testimony, my father would never get out of prison.

"Do you think Elizabeth would testify for my father if Jimmy were no longer a threat?" I asked him. "I don't know. She might be willing to testify against Jimmy as well if she knew it would put him away longer. She probably knows a lot more about his business too," he said. Both of us turned thoughtful. I knew there was no point in talking to her until Jimmy was arrested. She was afraid of him and with good reason. He had ruined her life as he did mine.

After breakfast, David got ready to go to the police station with the evidence he had collected. He had pictures and a recording of the transaction with the prostitute. They had also managed to get a list of names of women who were being used by Jimmy. He ran the escort service out of the casino hotel. Maybe one of these women could provide more evidence about Jimmy's business dealings.

David hugged me tightly before he left. "I won't be gone nearly as long this time," he told me. I was just glad that we were finally making progress. Hopefully, this was enough to arrest Jimmy. Standing in the middle of the room, I watched David walk out the door. I was alone once again.

I sat down on the bed and turned on the tv. There was nothing else to do. Staring at the screen, I was not really watching it. I was trying to keep my mind blank and not think. If I started thinking, I would start worrying. So instead, I watched the people on the screen. The noise from the tv was an added distraction from the empty room around me.

I glanced at the clock a while later and realized almost two hours had gone by. Then I turned my attention back to the tv. A while later, I heard a key in the door and felt an involuntary sigh of relief. I quickly stood from the bed. As the door swung open, my eyes opened wide in shock and I felt my body trembling. Two men entered the room and one had a gun pointed at me. They were the same two men that had been at the café in Salina.

"You will come with us," the man with the gun said, but my feet were frozen in place. I could not make myself move. He walked towards me and I took a step back, feeling the bed against the back of my legs. He grabbed my arm and pulled me towards the door. I struggled to pull out of his grasp, but it was useless. He was too strong.

When we got outside, I looked around the parking lot. There was no one around. "Don't even think about screaming. The consequences would be painful," the man holding my arm said. I believed him, and it was enough to make me bite my lip to stay silent. He pulled me towards a car and opened the back door. Then he pushed me inside and got in beside me, closing the door behind him. The other man got into the driver's seat and soon he had the car on the road.

There was no point in trying to get answers from either of the men. I knew I would get my answers from either my Uncle Jimmy or my grandfather. I knew that was where we were going. Turning to look out the window, I tried not to think about what could happen to me. I thought about David instead.

Neither of the men attempted to talk to me, but the man beside me kept the gun pointed at me the whole time. I did not pay attention to where we were going. I knew I would not recognize any of it. I knew from the road signs that we were heading into Denver, but nothing was familiar to me.

When I finally felt the car slowing down, I saw that we turned into a driveway. I looked up at the house in front of us and gasped, my jaw dropping open. It was my house. Jimmy had me brought to my house. I did not try to fight the man when his hand went around my arm once more. He pulled me from the car, and we walked towards the house.

Looking up at the house, I realized it was just as big as I remembered it. There was a man standing by the front door, and he opened the door as we approached. I noticed the gun in the holster on his hip. Then we stepped inside.

I was overwhelmed with memories as I looked around the rooms we walked through. Everything looked the same but different. The furniture was all new and the walls were painted in different colors than I remembered, but the house was the same. I quickly realized where we were headed. My father's office.

Chapter 14

When the other man opened the office door, the man holding my arm led me inside. Jimmy sat in the chair behind the desk. It was the same desk that had been here when I lived here. My father's desk. However, the man behind the desk had changed. He looked more like I remembered my grandfather. Gray was sprinkled throughout his dark hair, and lines had formed on his face. His expression was one of authority, and I felt a chill run up my spine.

His eyes never left mine as I was led to a chair in front of the desk and was pushed into it. He stood and turned to the wall behind him, opening the panel in the wall and revealing the safe. I watched as he entered the combination into the keypad and realized it was my birthday. That was definitely a combination no one else would guess, and I wondered why he had chosen it.

Jimmy reached into the safe and pulled out a stack of bills. He handed the money to the man that had brought me here. "Thank you, Charles. I'll be in touch when I need you again," Jimmy told the man. The man called Charles took the money and left the room, closing the door behind him. Jimmy sat back down in the chair behind the desk and we were alone. I was filled with dread.

"My dear, you have evaded us for quite a long time. I also have to say that you look just like your mother. Dad will be incredibly pleased," he told me. "Victor is still alive?" I asked him in surprise, unable to stop myself. "Yes, he is still alive, but he is not doing well. Knowing that you have come home will boost his spirits," he answered me.

"Why did you bring me here?" I asked him. "Aurora, certainly you know the answer to that question, and I am surprised you asked it. You belong here. You should have been raised here by us," he replied, and I shook my head no. "You took my family away from me," I told him, anger and fear making me bold.

"We are your family. It was unfortunate what happened to your mother, but she did not want to be a part of this family. Dad disowned her and gave her an ultimatum that she did not comply with. Her death was a result of that," he said calmly with no emotion in his voice. It was as if we were discussing a menu for dinner instead of my mother's murder, and I felt my body trembling in fear.

I gripped the arms of the chair. There were a lot of things that I wanted to say, but I wanted to survive even more. "So, you are going to keep me here against my will?" I asked, hearing the panic in my voice but trying to control it. "And where would you go if I let you leave? Back to your café in Kansas? Working long hours with nothing to show for it? Here we will take care of you. You will have everything you need and everything you want," he told me.

At least I knew I would not be dying any time soon, but I was beginning to think that Jimmy was crazy. I just had to bide my time and play along. I would have to show some resistance because Jimmy would expect that, but at my first opportunity, I would run. Jimmy's voice broke into my thoughts.

"Would you like to see the house? It has been nineteen years since you have been here. Let me show you around. I even had your old bedroom made up for you in anticipation of your arrival," he said. All I could do was nod. I really did want to see the house and the room that had been mine so many years ago.

Jimmy stood and walked around the desk. Then he held out his hand to me. The thought of touching him made my stomach crawl, but I reached out my hand to his. Together, we walked out of his office. The dining room looked the same except for the fresh paint that was a different color. The table was the same one where I had eaten so many meals with my parents. I ran my hand over the back of the chair that had been mine and looked around the room.

Next, we walked into the kitchen. We had a cook when I lived here, and I had not come into the kitchen very often. I could tell the cabinets had all been replaced, and the room had a modern look that I did not remember. We walked out of the kitchen and headed towards the stairs.

I could picture my mother and father standing by the stairs the evening they went to the gala. My feet stopped moving and I was frozen in that spot in the middle of the room. I did not even realize that tears were falling until Jimmy turned and looked at me. He reached up and wiped the tears away. "I bet it feels good to be home," he said softly.

I could not look at him and turned my head away. On the far wall were the two columns I remembered. They were built into the wall so that only half of the columns stuck out from the wall. A window was in the wall between them and a small table sat in front of the window. Padded armchairs were on either side of the table.

I felt Jimmy tug on my hand and I finally looked over at him. "Come on. Your grandfather is waiting," he said, and I let myself be pulled towards the stairs. Jimmy did not let go of my hand as we approached the room that had been my parents. I wondered what I would find on the other side of the door.

Jimmy opened the door and we entered what had once been my parents' sitting room. There was no one in this room and I looked around at the changes that had been made. Then Jimmy was pulling me towards the bedroom door. I took several deep breaths, trying to calm my beating heart as we walked across the room. Jimmy opened the door to the bedroom and led me inside.

The room was dark, and no lights were on. The curtains were closed, and very little light came in from behind them. "Dad, I've brought someone to see you," Jimmy said, and I noticed the form on the bed move. Jimmy let go of my hand and walked towards the bed, turning on a lamp that sat on the table next to the bed.

I looked down at the man lying on the bed. He was much older, and his hair was completely gray, but I recognized him. My breath caught in my throat and I did not even realize that I took a step back. Jimmy was quickly by my side, and his hand on my back pushed me forward until I was standing next to the bed looking down at my grandfather.

I looked at his face and it seemed hollow. There was no color in his cheeks and his skin seemed gray. His eyes studied me, and I was afraid to speak. "Abigail?" he asked softly. "No, Dad, this is Aurora," I heard Jimmy say from behind me. "Aurora," my grandfather whispered, his eyes never leaving mine. "Come here," he said, gesturing with his hand for me to come closer. Jimmy pushed me forward so that I was sitting on the edge of the bed beside Victor.

My grandfather reached up slowly until his hand rested on my arm. I felt a shudder go through my body at his touch. "You are really here," he said, and I saw his lips turn up into a smile. I looked up at Jimmy, unsure of what to do or say. He had a smile on his face as he looked at his father. "I told you I would find her," he said. "You are home," my grandfather said to me. All I could think about was getting out of this room and away from this man.

I realized then that I hated him. I hated him for killing Annie and my mother. He had taken both of my parents away from me. I looked up at Jimmy and I hated him too. I was grateful that my father had hidden me away from them and did not want to think about the life I would have had if I had been raised by these men.

"Dad, you rest, and I will bring Aurora to see you again later," Jimmy said. Then he motioned for me to follow him as he walked towards the door. I did not hesitate to stand from the bed, anxious to get away from this man and his touch on my arm. I knew I had to get away from here, away from this house, but I did not know how.

I followed Jimmy through the sitting room and back out to the hallway. We were heading to my room now. Jimmy opened the door to what had been my sitting room so many years ago, and he motioned for me to enter in front of him. I stepped through the doorway. As I looked around the room, I was overwhelmed with emotions and memories.

Chapter 15

The carpet in this room had been replaced and the walls were painted a different color. There were no toys or shelves of games along the walls. I had spent many hours in this room with Annie. The table that we had eaten meals on was gone, and a love seat, two armchairs, and two end tables were the only furniture in the room.

I could remember playing board games with Annie at the table that had been in front of the window. I remembered crawling across the floor laughing, with Annie crawling after me, knowing that if she caught me, she would tickle me. She had let me borrow one of her t-shirts once. It had been more like a gown on me. Then she let me paint with real paint and brushes at the table.

The brushes had been awkward in my hands, and it had turned into finger painting. I had gotten so much paint on Annie's shirt, but she had not cared. I turned to the corner where a bookshelf had once stood. Annie had read to me every day, and I had loved those moments of getting lost in a story.

Memories flooded my head as I looked around the room. Jimmy stood silently, just watching me. Finally, I stepped slowly towards the bedroom door. I opened it and walked into my bedroom. The furniture was all different, but the bed was in the same position that my bed had been in so many years ago.

I could picture myself in that bed and my father and mother leaning over me to say goodnight. I could picture Annie crawling into the bed beside me because I was afraid to go to sleep. Then I remembered why I had been afraid, and I now knew that those fears had been justified. I turned to face Jimmy.

"Will you please give me some time alone?" I asked softly, not trusting my voice to say anything more. I was grateful when Jimmy agreed and stepped out of the room. I laid down on the bed and curled up in a ball and cried. I cried for what had been taken away from me. I cried for the uncertainty of my future, and I cried because of the fear that I felt.

When I was out of tears, I stayed in the same position on the bed. I closed my eyes and pictured David. I wondered if he had made it back to the motel yet and found that I was gone. I wondered what he would do and if he would be able to find me. He would know that Jimmy had found me and taken me.

A long time later, I heard a knock on the door. I sat up on the bed and looked at the door as it opened. A woman stood in the doorway and she gave me a tender smile. She was much older than me, and I wondered if this was Jimmy's wife. I knew he had been married and had a daughter my age, but that was all I knew about him.

The woman walked towards the bed, and I watched her as she approached. "Aurora, my name is Marybeth. It is so good to finally meet you. Jimmy is my husband and we have been anxiously awaiting your arrival. Do you like your room?" she asked me kindly. I was not sure what to say so I just nodded. She smiled down at me.

"I am sure you are probably hungry. It is a little later than we usually eat lunch, but we held off so that you could join us," she said, the smile still on her face. "If you will follow me, lunch is ready," she continued. I did not know what else to do, so I stood from the bed and followed her out of the room.

When we entered the dining room, Jimmy was already seated at the table. He was sitting at the end where my father used to sit. There were only place settings for three people, and Jimmy looked up at me and pointed to one of the chairs. I made myself walk forward and sit down. This whole situation was awkward and unsettling for me, but both Jimmy and Marybeth acted as if I joined them frequently for meals. I felt like we were all playing house.

The two of them chatted about their day and a few minutes later a lady entered the room with dishes of food. My stomach growled when I smelled the aroma from the food. I was hungry, but I was in turmoil and did not know if I would be able to eat anything. I reminded myself that I had to go along with this until I could find my chance to escape, and I knew that I did not want to starve. I would at least have to eat something.

I sat on Jimmy's left, and Marybeth sat across from me on Jimmy's right. Her smile seemed to be permanently attached to her face, and I wondered about that. She had obviously been married to Jimmy for a long time, and I wondered if she knew that he ran a prostitution ring. Luckily, the two of them seemed content to talk to each other and they let me keep to my own thoughts.

Jimmy filled my plate from the dishes on the table and then he filled his plate and started eating. Marybeth filled her own plate. I reached for my fork and took a bite, hoping my stomach would not revolt. I was grateful when I realized my stomach was cooperating with the food that I was forcing in it.

When I had eaten as much as I thought I could, I put my fork down and placed my hands in my lap. Jimmy turned in his chair and looked at me. I could not help the question that came from my mouth. "How did you find me?" I asked him, and he laughed. I did not know what that laugh meant, but it made my heart skip a beat and my breath caught in my throat while I anxiously waited for him to answer.

"Well, there's this small quaint town outside of Denver. It has a beautiful backdrop of the mountains. It is a perfect tourist trap. I am in the process of building a resort there," he said, and my jaw dropped open. "I have already purchased the land, and if everything goes as planned, we should begin construction in another month or two," he continued.

"I have people in that town. They saw you there with that reporter and heard that he was asking questions. Anyone that knew your mother would know that you are her daughter. Even my father thought you were Abigail," he explained. David had been right. I should have stayed at the motel.

I looked down at my plate and could not look back up at my uncle. "You will be happy here," he said gently. "With your family where you belong. I understand that this will be an adjustment for you, and it will take time. You may go anywhere in the house you want. If you want a midnight snack, the kitchen is available. However, you will not leave this house," he said firmly.

"There is a security system and every door and window are secure. I have security outside of the house at all times. If you attempt to leave, they will know. And if you attempt to leave, there will be consequences," he said. I could tell by the tone of his voice that he was serious. I did not know how or when, but I knew I would be leaving here. I just needed to figure out how.

When both Jimmy and Marybeth were finished eating, they stood from the table. "I will be in my office," Jimmy said, and left the room. "So, what do you want to do?" Marybeth asked me as I stood from my chair. The smile was still on her face. I thought for a moment about how to reply.

"It has been a difficult day. I think I will just go to my room now," I replied. I did not wait for a response and I turned and quickly left the room before she could stop me. I hurried up the stairs and into my sitting room and sat down on the couch. My mind wandered, and I thought about my parents and Annie.

I had no tears left to cry, and I stared at nothing as my thoughts drifted back to a long time ago. My dream from the night before came to mind. Then I tried to remember that night at the carnival. My mother and I had eaten hot dogs. She had already purchased tickets so that we could ride the rides, so when we were done eating, we got in the line for the tilt-a-whirl.

I remembered our security was standing not too far away. Closing my eyes, I tried to picture everything that I had seen. My mother and I rode the ride, then got back into the line to ride again. That was when I saw him. Jimmy really had been there. He was watching us…no, he was watching me. I opened my eyes and stood from the couch.

Quickly, I left my room and headed down the stairs. When I reached the bottom, I turned and headed towards my father's office. I did not knock but opened the door and walked inside. Jimmy was sitting at his desk and he looked up at me startled. "Aurora," he said in surprise.

"You were there, weren't you?" I asked him. My fists were balled at my side and I was breathing heavily. My heart was beating rapidly, and my adrenaline was pumping through my body. "I was where, Aurora?" he asked me calmly. "The carnival. The night my mother was murdered. You were there. It wasn't Victor, it was you that had her killed," I accused him. I noticed the smile that formed on his lips, and a chill went up my spine.

"I did what had to be done. My father has killed many people, but he could not bring himself to get rid of his precious Abigail. Even though he taught me that disowned meant dead, he would not do it. So, I took care of it myself. It just worked out that your father was heading that way, and someone saw his car leaving. I knew he had found you afterwards, but framing him was the ultimate satisfaction for me," he said. His voice held no emotion, and definitely not anything that could be mistaken for regret.

"You are a monster!" I screamed at him and ran out of the room. I could hear his laughter behind me. I did not stop running until I was in my room, and I collapsed on the bed. This could not be my life. I would not be able to survive living here for long. I was a prisoner, no different than a caged animal. A terrified caged animal.

Chapter 16

I had no doubt that he would follow through with consequences if I tried to escape, and I knew I did not want to find out what those consequences were. The man that brought me here had promised me pain if I screamed. There was no doubt in my mind that Jimmy had a wide range of "consequences" that he was familiar with.

I stood from the bed and walked into my sitting room. On the wall across from the couch were the two large windows where my table used to be. I slid the curtains open on one window and stood in front of it. If David were looking for me, he might come here. This was my only hope as the hours passed and I watched the street.

My rooms were on the right side of the house, and from the windows in here and in my bedroom, I could see down one direction of the road that ran in front of the house. It was a good distance between this house and the next one, and I knew that no one there could help me. I leaned my forehead against the glass and closed my eyes.

David had to find me. It was the only way that I would escape.

Marybeth came to my room when dinner was ready, and I followed her down the stairs to the dining room. Marybeth and Jimmy conversed throughout the whole meal, but I was grateful that they again did not try to include me. I ate very slowly, the fear and hate inside of me making my hands shake.

When dinner was done, Jimmy told me goodnight. I was glad that I could go back to my room and not have to worry about seeing him again until the morning. When I got to my room, I resumed my position from earlier at the window. I leaned my head against the glass and closed my eyes. I would not need to see David. I just needed him to see me.

When it was dark outside, I continued to stand at the window. The light in the room behind me would make me even more visible to someone outside. I was not tired, but my body was exhausted. There was a heavy weight on my chest and my breathing was erratic. What I was feeling was hopelessness. Standing at this window was the only hope I had, and I knew it was slim.

Finally, I felt as if my legs would give out and I turned from the window. I walked into the bedroom and looked around. When I opened one of the drawers in the dresser, I realized it was filled with clothes. I pulled out a t-shirt and held it up. It was my size. I examined the rest of the drawers, and then looked in the closet. It was full of clothes as well.

I got undressed and slipped the t-shirt on. Then I walked into the bathroom. Everything I would need was in here. There was an unopened toothbrush and some toothpaste, shampoo, soap, deodorant, and a brush. I sighed deeply and opened the toothbrush and brushed my teeth.

When I was back in my room, I pulled the blankets back on the bed and crawled into it. The room was too quiet, so I reached for the tv remote and turned the tv on. I turned the volume down low, then laid back on the pillow. Fear kept me staring at the ceiling for a long time. I knew the dreams would return tonight, and I thought about Annie.

When I woke in a panic, it was still dark outside. I did not think I had been asleep for long. The dream of the carnival had returned. I got out of the bed and turned my light on and walked to the window. I opened the curtains and leaned my head against the glass. With the light on, I could not see anything through the window except my reflection and the reflection of the room around me, but still I stood there.

I did not see the shadow move across the lawn a good distance from the house. My eyes were closed, and I thought of David. He had to find me. I could not endure another day in this house. Finally, I turned from the window and shut the light off. I crawled back into the bed and pulled the covers up around me.

I laid in bed for another thirty minutes. It was only 3:00 in the morning, but I did not think I could sleep again. Slowly, I got out of bed and slipped on a pair of shorts. Then I walked out of my room and out of the sitting room to the hallway. The house was completely quiet as I walked down the hallway towards the stairs. There were no sounds in the house, and I knew everyone was asleep. I made my way down the stairs. Because I was barefoot, it was easy to keep my footsteps quiet on the marble floor as I made my way to my father's office.

I gently opened the door, turning the knob slowly to not make any noise. I stepped inside the office and looked around, then walked around the desk and opened the panel on the wall. I entered the combination of the safe. When I heard the click, I pulled the door open. There was only a small amount of light coming in the window from the streetlights outside, but I reached inside the safe and felt around.

There was a stack of files and what felt like a leather-bound book. I could feel stacks of money, but I skipped over those. I picked up the book and walked to the window for more light. When I opened the book and flipped through the pages, I knew this was what we had been looking for. I had to hide it until I could get it out of the house.

I closed the safe and made my way quietly to the column that I had hid behind when I was five. Pulling on the column, it did not budge. I closed my eyes and tried to remember the night that Annie had put me inside. Obviously, my parents had told Annie about the column, but I had not known about it until she opened it.

I remembered Annie reaching up to where the column met the wall on one side, and I lifted my hand to around the same place she had. Running my fingers up and down the corner, I felt when my fingers pushed on a spot that gave out. I heard the click in the column and pulled it open. Quickly, I set the book inside on the floor and closed the column. Then I ran back upstairs to my room.

When I woke the next morning, I realized that it was after 11:00 in the morning. The dream had not returned, and I was grateful. My next thought went to the book I had found. I hoped that Jimmy did not know about the column. It was not exactly something that could be easily stumbled upon, but if he did find it, I knew I would have to endure his wrath. I shuddered at the thought. Well, it was too late now.

I grabbed some clothes from the dresser and headed to the bathroom for a shower. When I was dressed, I headed downstairs to find something to eat. Hopefully, I could get some lunch before Jimmy and Marybeth had their meal so I would not have to sit at the table with them. I did not want to sit through that again.

When I got to the bottom of the stairs, I did not see anyone around. I walked into the kitchen and saw the lady that had brought our food to the table yesterday. She was chopping some vegetables. She smiled when she looked up at me. "Um, is there something I can eat? I kind of slept through breakfast," I said hesitantly, not sure if she would appreciate my presence in the kitchen.

"Sure. Check the fridge and see if you find something. The pantry is behind that door," she said kindly, pointing with the knife in her hand. I walked towards the fridge and opened it. Grabbing a yogurt and an apple, I asked the woman about silverware. She pointed again. I grabbed a spoon from the drawer she indicated and took the food to my room.

I once again stood in front of the window while I ate. There was not much to look at, and I had seen this view hundreds of times since this had been my bedroom. Grabbing one of the armchairs next to the couch, I dragged it across the room to the window. There was no point in standing so long. I was deep in thought when I heard a knock on the door, and it made me jump.

When the door opened, it was Marybeth. I wondered if they had left the house earlier and had just gotten home. "Jimmy would like to see you in his office," she said, the smile still firmly planted on her face. I nodded and stood from the chair, wondering if my uncle had discovered the book was missing from the safe. As long as he did not know about the column, I knew he would never find it.

Marybeth opened the office door and I stepped inside. She closed the door behind me. I looked over at Jimmy sitting behind my father's desk and felt my anger return. The anger would keep me alert, and I waited for Jimmy to speak. He stood and walked around the desk until he was standing in front of me. He just looked at me for several moments.

"Something went missing from my safe last night," he told me. My eyes never left his, but I did not speak. "I have a feeling that you are the one who took it," he said. I was not prepared for the hand that swung up and slapped me. My head jerked to the side and my hand went to my cheek. It burned and felt like it was on fire.

"I want it back," he said, his voice controlled. "I don't know what you are talking about," I told him. My eyes had filled with tears from the sting and I did not try to look at him. "I think you are lying to me. Right now, I have people searching your rooms, and when they find it, you will be punished," he told me.

"I didn't take anything," I replied desperately. This was the story I was sticking to and I had to make it convincing. "I was in my room all night. I couldn't sleep and I watched tv for hours. I didn't even wake up until 11:00 this morning," I explained to him. I waited for him to reply, unsure of what he would do next, but hoping he would not slap me again.

"If that is true, then I will apologize, but not until your room is searched. I do not trust you. If they do not find it, then I will believe you. You may go now, but do not go upstairs," he told me. I quickly opened the door and stepped out of his office. Once the door was closed, I breathed a sigh of relief.

Chapter 17

I made my way through the rooms of the house, stopping every once in a while to look out a window or examine the paintings and pictures on the walls. I had just walked into the large dining room and was looking at some China in a hutch when Jimmy walked into the room. I took a step back from him as he approached, but I felt the wall behind my back.

"Aurora, I must apologize. They did not find it in your room. I am sorry for hitting you. However, that is a mild punishment if you cross me. It would do well for you to keep that in mind," he said. Then he reached up and touched my cheek where he had slapped me. The familiar chill went up my spine and I turned my head away from his touch. He dropped his hand.

"Dinner is at 6:30. I will expect to see you there," he said. It was not a request but a command, and I knew I would be there on time. I did not want to anger him again. He turned and left the room, but I waited a few minutes before I walked out. I did not want to run into him again.

When I reached the stairs, I heard voices coming from Jimmy's office. The door was open, and I could hear Jimmy's voice was angry and out of control. I hurried up the stairs not wanting to be on the other end of his wrath again. I sat down in the chair in front of the window and stayed there until it was time for dinner.

Dinner was tense and even Marybeth did not try to talk to Jimmy. Her smile faltered a few times, but she made sure it was there when she looked over at me. I did not try to engage either of them in conversation. I concentrated on my plate and the food on it. Time seemed to slow down and I could not wait for this meal to be over.

After dinner, I returned to my room. My jail cell. The only difference in this and a real jail cell was mine was comfortable. I sat down in the chair in front of the window. Being in this house was making me depressed. When the sun set and it grew dark outside, I stayed in the chair. I had to let David see me. He had to come for me.

The house grew quiet and I was glad that no one had come to check on me after dinner. I stared at my reflection in the glass and I thought about my father. This, what I was feeling, had been his life for nineteen years, only his time had been spent in prison. I had to get away, and I had to save him.

When I stood and walked into the bedroom, I saw that it was 2:30 in the morning. That is when the idea came to me. Obviously, I was tired, and probably not thinking rationally. I was an emotional wreck. I knew that this would be difficult, and I did not know if I would even fit. However, I knew I had to try. I used the bathroom then left my room, shutting the door quietly behind me.

When I made my way down the stairs, I walked into the kitchen first. It was dark, but I had seen the bread in the pantry. I walked towards the pantry door and opened it. I grabbed a few slices of bread out of the package and left the kitchen. Walking towards the column on the right, I reached up and pushed at the corner of the wall, releasing the latch that held the column closed.

When the column opened, I reached down and picked up the book, tucking it into the waistband of my shorts and pulling my shirt down over it. Then I turned and backed inside. There was a small handle on the inside of the column, and I pulled it closed around me. It was a tight fit, but the column closed. I closed my eyes tightly, remembering the last time I had been inside here.

I felt the panic beginning to bubble up inside of me, but I pictured David in my head and focused on breathing evenly. I pushed against the column and found that it was firmly in place. That was good. It meant I could lean against it. Now, I just had to wait. I did not know what I was going to accomplish by this except to anger my uncle, but if I stayed hidden it would be worth it.

I do not know how I managed to fall asleep standing up except that the space was too small for me to fall over. I woke to the sound of voices. Angry voices. I listened intently and could hear my uncle's voice. "She couldn't have gotten out of the house. I want everyone looking for her until she is found," I heard him say. I have no idea how much time passed, but I felt the smile on my face a long while later when he was informed that I was gone. "Impossible!" I heard him yell. "Somebody is going to pay for this," he said.

I had shoved the bread slices into the pocket of my shorts, and I pulled them out and started eating one. I had not brought a drink because I did not want to have a need to go to the bathroom. That would just be more torture. It was bad enough being in total darkness. I ate one slice of the bread and put the rest back in my pocket. I leaned my head against the column and just listened to the noises and voices on the other side.

I drifted in and out of sleep. Sometimes the house got quiet and sometimes there was all kinds of activity just on the other side of the column. Obviously, my uncle did not know about the column, and as long as I stayed inside, I was safe. I heard numerous voices that I had not heard before, and everyone seemed to be in a panic. I smiled to myself.

I had no idea how long I had been hiding. My eyes remained closed the whole time, but I still had to focus on my breathing several times as I felt myself begin to panic in the darkness. The voices on the other side of the column helped calm me some, just by reminding me that I was not completely alone. It was comforting and helped keep me hidden, knowing that I could step out of the column at any time.

When my stomach growled at me again, I ate another piece of bread. I had one left, but I would get more after everyone went to bed. The only problem with that is that I would have no idea when nighttime came. I guess once the house got quiet, I would just wait a long time before coming out.

My legs were beginning to ache, and I put all of my weight on one foot to relieve the other one for a while. I switched back and forth for a long time. It gave me something to do to relieve the boredom. Sometimes I leaned against the wall and sometimes I stood straight. I could only bend my knees slightly before they touched the column in front of me.

A long time later, after I ate the last piece of bread, I wondered what time it was and how long I had been in here. Suddenly, I heard another set of voices. It sounded like David, but I was not sure. Then I heard my uncle's voice. "Officer, there is no girl here. You can look around if you would like," he said.

"I know she's here. I saw her in the upstairs window," David said. I felt around the inside of the column trying to find something to release the column, but there was nothing. I had not considered that once I got inside I might not be able to open it from in here. Now I could not stop myself from panicking. I had to get out.

I lifted my hands and pounded on the column. Balling my fists, I pounded harder and I yelled David's name. He had found me, but now I could not get to him. It felt like I was hyperventilating, and I could not get my voice to work anymore. I continued to pound on the column, hoping that he could hear me, but not having enough room to gather momentum in my fists to pound any harder.

"Aurora, are you okay?" I heard David say, just on the other side of the panel. I could not speak, so I just continued to pound. It seemed like forever until the column opened in front of me and I fell forwards. David caught me and lowered me to the floor. I could not breathe, and I could not stand.

"Aurora, breathe. Just breathe slowly. You are safe," I heard him say from above me. My chest hurt and my heart was pounding. I kept my eyes tightly closed, knowing the light would be too much. The light that was coming through my eyelids was already almost painful.

David continued to speak softly to me, and I focused on the sound of his voice. His hands rubbed up and down my arms, his touch soothing. I reached forward and grabbed the front of his shirt. I needed to feel that he was there because I could not see him.

I could hear other voices around me, but I focused only on David's voice. When I could finally breathe deeply, I sat up and reached for his hands. "How long were you in there?" he asked me softly, and I could hear the concern in his voice. "Since before 3:00 in the morning," I told him. I could hear his sharp intake of breath.

I heard footsteps on the marble floor approach us, and I clung to David. He was kneeling on the floor beside me, and I had turned my head into his chest to blot out some of the light. "Officer, I'm going to take her back to our motel room and let her get some sleep. I'll bring her to the station in the morning," David said. "That's fine. We will take care of this," I heard the other man say.

"Do you think you can walk?" David asked me softly. "I'm not sure," I told him. He took both of my hands and pulled me to my feet. I took a step, but my leg buckled, and David caught me. The next thing I knew, he was picking me up and carrying me across the room. I wrapped my arms around his neck and turned my face into his chest once again to block out the light.

I could tell when we stepped out of the house because the light went away. "What time is it?" I asked him. "Almost 10:00 at night," David replied. I had been hiding for nineteen hours. I slowly tried opening my eyes, and it took quite a long time for my eyes to adjust so that I could make out shapes around me.

I could see David's car in the driveway and several police cars. I had to squint my eyes and look away from the flashing lights. David set me down beside the car and I held onto him for support as he opened the door. He helped me down to the seat and shut the door behind me.

Chapter 18

It took about forty minutes to get to the motel, but I had never been so happy to see it. David did not even let me attempt to use my legs and lifted me from the seat of the car. When he got the door to the room open, he walked to my bed and set me down on it. Then he walked to the fridge and opened it. I watched him as he pulled items out of the fridge.

When he walked back to me, he handed me a plate with a sandwich. "Thank you," I said softly. I had never seen David so quiet, his expression still full of concern. Neither of us had spoken a word on the drive here, and I wondered what he was thinking. I would have asked, but I was much too hungry. So, I picked up the sandwich and took a bite.

David handed me a bottle of water and I drank half of it before I set it down on the table beside the bed. I finished the sandwich and the rest of the water, then looked over at David where he was sitting on the edge of his bed. We both watched each other for a few moments.

"What are you thinking?" I asked him softly, not able to read the expression on his face now. He did not answer me for a long time. Finally, he spoke. "I keep remembering coming back to the room and you were gone. I didn't know what had happened or where you were," he said, and I could hear the emotion in his voice. I stood and managed to take one step over and sit down on the bed next to him.

"You found me," I told him, my hand reaching up to his cheek. "You are the only reason I survived. Whenever I started to panic, I thought of you. When I was inside the column, and it was pitch black, I closed my eyes and pictured your face. You were there with me," I told him gently.

"When I was in my room, I stood in front of the window for hours, both day and night, hoping you would see me. Hoping you would find me," I continued. "I did see you," he said softly. My eyes opened wide in surprise. "That was the only thing that gave me hope," I replied. "That you would find me."

"It was dark outside, and I knew you could not see me. But I knew that you were there waiting for me to find you. That is when I went back to the police. I had seen you and I knew you were there, but it took a lot of convincing before they would agree to go and look for you," he told me. Then he reached his arm around me and I laid my head against his chest. This felt so right.

"Come on," he finally said. "You need some sleep." Before I stood from the bed, I pulled up my shirt and grabbed the book from the waistband of my shorts. I held it out to David. "What's this?" he asked me. "It's evidence," I told him. He set the book down on the table beside the bed. "Tomorrow," he said gently.

I stood up and stepped across to my bed and pulled the blankets back. When I crawled into the bed, I moved to the other side. I looked over at David. "Please?" I asked him hesitantly. "I haven't been able to sleep. Nightmares," I whispered, feeling the same fear I had as a child when Annie would lay down with me.

David did not hesitate to get into the bed beside me. He pulled the covers up over us and reached his arm under me, so my head was laying on his shoulder. I turned towards him and wrapped my arm around his middle. He pressed a kiss to the top of my head, and I closed my eyes.

When I woke the next morning, I could see the light shining through the crack in the curtain and I knew it was late in the morning. David was not beside me or in his bed, and I looked around the room until my eyes found him. He was standing across the room by the door with the book I had given him last night open in his hands. I watched him for several moments and smiled to myself. David had become everything to me.

"Anything good in that book?" I asked him, and he looked over at me and grinned. "This is the jackpot," he said excitedly. "Well, don't let me distract you. I'm going to go take a shower," I told him, grinning back at him. He shut the book and walked towards me and held out his hand. How quickly I had forgotten that I had been hiding in a column for nineteen hours the day before.

I swung my legs over the bed and reached for his hand before I stood. When I was on my feet, I took a tentative step. Thank goodness my legs were back to normal. I whispered a sigh of relief and looked up at

David. "David," I said softly, but was not yet ready to say what I had on my mind.

"What is it, Aurora?" he asked me gently. His hand caressed my cheek as we stood watching each other. I wanted to memorize the features of his face in case we were ever separated again. It really was not necessary as I had easily brought his face to mind when I was in that column.

"Jimmy was there," I finally said. "Yes, we got him," David replied with a look of confusion on his face. "No, I don't mean at the house. I mean at the carnival. He was there, and he was watching me. It wasn't Victor. Victor could not bring himself to do it, so Jimmy killed my mother," I told him.

"You go take a shower, and we will tell the police everything," he said gently. I nodded my head and turned towards the bathroom. When I finished my shower and walked out of the bathroom, David was sitting at the table with the book open in front of him. He was taking notes in a journal. I smiled as I watched him. He was very intent and did not see me approach until I was standing beside him.

I laid my hand on his shoulder and he looked up at me and gave me a beautiful smile. "I'm taking notes. I have a feeling once we turn this over to the police, I won't see it again. I want to make sure I have the story straight when I write it," he told me. I smiled down at him.

"David, should we get an attorney for dad first? We could let him look over all the evidence in case it disappears. We don't know how far Jimmy's reach goes. He could have friends in the police department. He has friends everywhere," I told him. I explained what Jimmy had told me about how he had found me. I could see David was thinking about what I said. "Let me make some calls," he replied.

Two hours later, we were in the car heading into Denver. My hand was in David's and that was comforting. I did not know what was going to happen or if the evidence we had would get my father out of prison. All I could do was worry and hope. I felt the gentle squeeze on my hand and looked over at David. "It's going to be okay," he said reassuringly. I managed half of a smile, then turned and looked out the window.

When we parked and headed into a tall building, I felt a chill run up my spine. David led me to the elevator and kept my hand firmly tucked in his. We got off on the fifth floor and walked down a hallway and stopped in front of a door. Michael W. Goldman, Attorney at Law was written on the frosted glass window. I looked up at David. "We can trust him. He was recommended to me by a close friend," David said.

Before we had left the motel, I had written in my journal. I added seeing Jimmy at the carnival and other memories that I had remembered. Then I wrote every detail I could remember about my kidnapping and my stay at Jimmy's house. I wrote down everything that he had said to me, and everything that he had admitted about killing my mother. I held that journal in my hands, and David held the leather-bound book as we walked in the door of the attorney's office.

It was just a few minutes of waiting before we were led to a conference room. A few minutes after that, an older man entered the room and introduced himself as Michael Goldman. We shook hands then took a seat at the large table in the room. When he heard my name, he looked at me with an intense look. I knew that he recognized my name.

"I will have to say that this is a surprise," the attorney started by saying. "For many years, people here have wondered if you were alive or dead," he said to me. "I am very much alive, as you can see, and my father did not kill my mother. That is why we are here. An innocent man is sitting in prison, and we need your help to get him out and put the guilty people away for a long time," I told him.

Chapter 19

For the next two and a half hours, we poured over the information in my journal and in the book. When we were finished, David and I looked up at the attorney to see what he would say. "I believe the evidence here is sufficient to have your father released and to put Jimmy Smaldone away for a long time," he told us. "Leave these two books with me and I will make sure they are filed as evidence," he continued.

"We are heading to the police station next," David told him. "They need to get Aurora's statement about the kidnapping." The attorney reached for the phone on the desk and hit a button. A woman's voice came through the intercom. "Helen, reschedule any appointments I have for the rest of the day. I will be out of the office," he said. "Yes, sir," she replied.

He looked back at us. "I don't want this turning into an interrogation. Especially if Mr. Smaldone does have friends on the force. We will go, and I will do most of the talking," he told us. We shook hands again and he looked at me with the same intense expression he had had before. "This will all be over soon," he said in a gentle tone. I could only hope that he was right.

At the police station, we were led into an interrogation room. It looked just like the ones on tv. It was just the attorney and me. They had not let David come with us. An officer sat on the other side of the table, and my hands shook in my lap. "Why don't you start at the beginning," the officer said. I looked over at the attorney.

"The initial attempt at kidnapping Miss Davis was in Salina, KS where she lives. Jimmy Smaldone sent two men to take her from her place of employment," the attorney informed the officer. "Her father placed her there with friends because at the time his wife was murdered, Aurora was not safe here. Her uncle and grandfather had attempted to kidnap her several times when she was a child."

"The same two men that had tried to take her in Salina entered her motel room three days ago and took her at gunpoint. She was taken to the house of Jimmy Smaldone where she was kept against her will for two days. During that time, he admitted to my client that he was the one responsible for her mother's death. Mr. Smaldone had her mother killed so that he could take my client as a child and raise her as part of his family. Those plans were thwarted when she escaped," the attorney explained.

I was so glad that I had not had to say anything yet. The attorney answered all of the officer's questions for me, and when the officer looked over at me, I just nodded my agreement. Suddenly, there was a knock on the door. When it opened, two men in suits walked inside. They introduced themselves as FBI agents, and told the officer that this interview was over. Then one of the agents looked at me.

"You will come with us," the agent said gently. I looked up at the attorney, afraid and not knowing what was happening. He leaned towards me. "I called them," he told me. "Go with them. They will keep you safe, and I will work on getting your father out," he said. I nodded and stood from my chair. I was trembling slightly as I walked down the hallway with the agents, one on each side of me.

When we entered the lobby, I saw David immediately. I ran to him and wrapped my arms around his waist, his arms crushing me against him. "What's going on?" I heard him say to the agents. "We are taking her into protective custody until we know she is safe," I heard one of the men say. I turned to look at the agents.

"What about David?" I asked them. "We are here to make sure you are safe. When that happens, you will be free to go," he said kindly. David kissed the top of my head. "I will go and talk with your father and let him know what is going on. I will get with Mr. Goldman. We will keep things moving here. I am not going anywhere," he said, his hand caressing my cheek. "Ma'am, we have to go now," one of the agents said. I looked up at David, refusing to say goodbye. This was not goodbye.

I stepped into the waiting car and soon we were leaving the police station. I watched out the window as we drove, wondering where we were headed. The two agents were in the front seat and I was in the back, so I was left alone with my thoughts. This all seemed to have gotten so complicated very quickly, and all I wanted to do was see my father and go back to David.

When the car finally stopped, we were in front of a grand hotel. When we walked through the doors, we did not stop at the counter but walked across the elegant lobby. The agents led me straight to the elevator and we got off on the eleventh floor. We walked down the hallway and stopped in front of a door. The agent held a key card to the door and opened it and we stepped inside.

The room was a suite and had a large living area with a couch and sofa chair. A glass coffee table was in front of the couch and two glass end tables were on either side. There was a full kitchen to our left and a bar with three bar stools. The agents led me forward and one of them opened a door to the bedroom. "You should be comfortable here," he told me sincerely. I nodded, not yet ready to speak.

I did not have a bag or any clothes, so there was no point in going into the bedroom. I turned and stepped towards the couch and sat down on one end. One agent sat down at the other end of the couch and the other one sat in the chair across from us. We all just looked at each other for a few moments, and I was not sure why I was even here. Finally, one of the agents spoke.

"We need for you to recount everything you remember. We have sent an agent to speak with your father, so we will be getting his version of what happened. But now we need yours. We have had Jimmy Smaldone on our radar for quite some time now, but we have not been able to find enough evidence against him to have him charged. It seems you have provided us with that. Now we need to hear everything. We would like to charge him with as much as possible. If he was responsible for your mother's death as well, we will help you get your father freed and make sure Jimmy pays for it," he told me.

I took a deep breath. This was going to take a while, but this seemed to be the only chance I had to see my father again. I started with my memory of when my mother and I went to the salon. I told them about being forced into the car and meeting my uncle and grandfather for the first time. I had been terrified, even before Jimmy had pulled a gun on us. I had had nightmares ever since.

Next, I told what I remembered of my parents before the gala. I described what they were wearing, and how they had both given me a hug and kiss goodbye. Then I told them about the games that Annie and I had played. When we heard glass breaking, Annie had shoved me into the column. I had heard three gunshots and my grandfather's voice. They were there searching for me and had killed Annie.

The next thing I told them about was the night of the carnival. I relayed what happened that night with as much detail as possible. When my father had found me, I had told him that my mother was dead. I could not remember much about that drive. It had seemed to last forever, and we had only stopped to use the bathroom and get gas. I remembered showing up at the farmhouse the next day and my father introducing me to my grandparents, even though now, I knew they were not related to me.

I skipped my years of growing up and explained how my father had sent David to watch me and make sure I was safe. Then I explained about the two men trying to take me from my job at the café and how David had helped me to escape. That was how we ended up back in Colorado. I had not been back here since I was five.

I told them about visiting the small town and how Jimmy's people had seen me there. It was the same two men from the café in Salina that had taken me from the motel at gunpoint. When I told about my two days at Jimmy's house, my body was trembling. I had been so afraid, and I remembered that fear. My hands were clasped together tightly in my lap.

I had recognized my birth date immediately when Jimmy entered it in the combination on the safe. Then I told them how I snuck downstairs in the middle of the night and hid the book in the column. I had spent hours of my day and night standing in front of my window hoping David would find me and see me so he would know I was there. When I told them of facing my fear of the dark and hiding in the column once again, they both had a look of amazement and respect on their faces. I felt my lips turn up in a smile.

"Where is this book now?" one of the agents asked me. "We were not sure who we could trust in the police department, so we handed it over to the attorney, Mr. Goldman. David had looked at it and he said it was a jackpot in taking down Jimmy and putting him away," I told him honestly.

One of the agents stood and paced the room. "When will I be able to see my father?" I asked softly. He turned to look at me, and I saw the smile spread across his face. "I have a feeling that it will be very soon," he told me, and that gave me hope. The agent then took a phone out of his pocket and stepped into the bedroom and shut the door behind him.

Chapter 20

The agents turned out to be pretty personable, and after the dinner they provided, we played cards at the table. We played until 10:00 p.m., and that must have been some ordained time for bedtime because one of the agents stacked the cards and they both told me good night. I did not know how good of a night this was going to be.

I headed into the bedroom dreading going to bed. There was an unopened hotel provided toothbrush in the bathroom, so I brushed my teeth and headed towards the bed. Realizing that the only bathroom was in here, that meant the agents would have to come through here if they needed to use it. I only hoped that I would be asleep so I would not notice them.

I crawled into the bed and thought about David. I wondered what he was doing or if he was back in the motel room. The more I thought about him, the more I felt the tension in my body dissipate. I closed my eyes and pictured him, knowing that I was dreading going to sleep without him here.

I was at the carnival and I was scared. Looking around, I did not see anyone I recognized. I spun in a circle, but the people around me were just talking and laughing and pointing out rides and games. People passed me, talking amongst themselves, and no one paid me any attention.

I saw the tilt-a-whirl, and I was filled with dread. Making my way to the ride, I watched carefully around me. That was when I saw them. The men with menacing expressions. I spun in a slow circle and realized they were all around me, advancing on me quickly from all sides. I was surrounded, and I tried to run, but I could not get away.

When they reached me, I could feel them pulling on my hair and clothes. They would not stop pinching and poking me. My body was on fire and I screamed in agony. Two firm hands gripped my shoulders and shook me, and I screamed again. Then I heard my name.

I opened my eyes wide and looked up at the man standing over me. I did not recognize him, and I felt another scream in my throat. "Aurora, you are safe. You had a nightmare," the man said. I burst into tears and rolled onto my side away from him. He sat down on the edge of the bed and rubbed my back in a soothing manner. When my tears subsided, I turned and looked up at him.

"I'm Agent Stements. We did a shift change at 11:00 last night. I will be here with you until morning," he told me softly. "What time is it?" I asked him, hearing my voice quiver. "Almost 2:30 in the morning. Can you go back to sleep?" he asked, and I quickly shook my head. I needed David. I needed to feel safe. I knew that I was, but it did not matter.

I stood from the bed and walked into the bathroom and splashed cold water on my face. Looking into the mirror, I studied my reflection. For some reason, I seemed to look different, but I did not know how or why. Something had changed. I wiped my face on a towel and walked back to the living room.

There was a second agent I did not recognize, and he introduced himself. "How long will I be here?" I asked them. "Hopefully, not long. Just a couple of days," Agent

Stements replied. I did not know if I could survive
without sleep for that long. I sighed deeply and sat down
on the couch.

Four days later, I heard a knock on the bedroom
door. "Come in," I called. I was already sitting up on the
bed with the tv playing softly. I had it on the weather
channel and was waiting for the weather report on
Kansas. It comforted me. An agent walked into the room
carrying a clothes bag. I looked up at him curiously.

So far, the agents had provided me with all of my
basic needs. This had included a few pairs of shorts and
jeans and some t-shirts. I looked at the bag he was
holding. "What is that for?" I asked him. "You have court
today," he said, and my jaw dropped open in surprise.

The agents had not yet provided me with any
details about either my father or my uncle. Usually, I did
not ask questions, but this time was different. "What am I
going to court for?" I asked hesitantly. "Your father's
retrial," he told me gently as a smile formed on his face.
"We have pulled some strings and got it moved up," he
said.

I quickly jumped from the bed and grabbed the bag from the agent. "Thank you," I said softly, and he nodded and left the room. In the bag was a pair of slacks and a blouse. I had never really owned any dressy clothes, but I did not stop to think about it as I got undressed and put the clothes on.

I glanced in the mirror and the image I saw definitely did not look like me. To me, I seemed older. Older than I had been when I left Salina just a couple of weeks ago. It seemed like I had been through a lifetime in those couple of weeks. I was anxious about seeing my father again after so long apart, but I knew David would be there as well.

When I walked into the living room, I sat down on the couch. The agents went over with me what to expect from court today. They reminded me to answer every question truthfully and explained how the prosecuting attorney and my attorney would both question me. My journal had been submitted as evidence along with the book I had taken from my uncle's house.

When it was time, I followed the agents out the door and to the elevator. They may have tried to tell me what to expect, but I was still apprehensive. When we pulled up to the courthouse, the sidewalk was filled with people. Reporters surrounded the car and my eyes opened wide as I looked at Agent Stements. He looked back at me from the front seat.

"We are going to get you inside the building as quickly as possible," he explained. "Do not answer any questions they ask you and do not talk to anyone. Understood?" he asked me, and I nodded. "Okay then, let's get you inside," he said. He opened his door and stepped out of the car.

When my door opened, Agent Stements reached for my hand and helped me from the car. The voices around me overwhelmed me and I could not have answered any questions even if I wanted to. All the voices blurred together until it just sounded like a loud noise rumbling in my ears.

Quickly, the other agent was on my other side, and they both held onto my arms as they propelled me forward through the throng of reporters. I kept my gaze straight ahead of me and did not make eye contact with anyone. We made our way up the stairs and into the building. That was when I saw David. I broke free of the agents' hands and ran to him.

I felt the air knocked out of my lungs from the force of my body hitting his, but I did not care. His arms were around me and that was all that mattered. The agents made their way to us but waited patiently for our reunion to be over. I looked up at David and he smiled down at me. "How have you been?" he asked me gently. "Just missing you," I replied honestly.

He kissed the top of my head. "Will you be inside?" I asked him. "No, the judge has ordered no reporters allowed. He doesn't want this to become the same circus that is going on outside," he told me. I was grateful that the crowd outside would not be there, but anxious because David would not be there either.

"It's going to be okay," he told me, smiling down at me and caressing my cheek with his hand. I leaned into his touch. "Besides, I have the inside scoop already," he said, and I grinned up at him. "We have to go inside now," Agent Stements told me. I looked up at David once more. "I will be right here when it is over," he assured me. I allowed the agents to lead me inside the court room.

I had never been inside a courtroom before and I was amazed by the room's opulence. There was no one else in the room, and the agents led me to one of the rows of benches towards the front. When the door we had come through opened again, I turned and saw Mr. Goldman enter the room. He saw us immediately and walked towards us, sitting down on the bench in front of us. He looked at me and smiled.

"Are you ready for this?" he asked me. "As ready as I will ever be, I suppose," I replied. "Don't worry," he told me. "We've got this," he said with a grin. He sounded much more confident than I felt, but that gave me hope. Hope was all I needed as I waited anxiously for the moment that I would see my father again.

Chapter 21

I watched as people filtered into the courtroom, and Mr. Goldman stood and walked towards the front of the courtroom and sat down at a large table on one side of the room. He opened his briefcase and pulled out stacks of paperwork. A long time later, I saw a door at the front open and the jury entered the court room. I knew that we would be starting soon.

The next person I saw come through that door was my father. I gasped when I saw him. He looked so much older than I remembered him, but he was clean cut and shaven and wore a suit. His eyes locked with mine, and I saw the tears falling down his cheeks, even at this distance. My breath caught in my throat and it was a few moments before I could inhale again.

He sat down in the chair beside Mr. Goldman, just a few yards in front of me, and I could not take my eyes off of him. When the bailiff had everyone stand, he announced the presence of the judge. My hands shook in my lap when we sat down again. Agent Stements reached over and put his hand over mine. I looked up at him and he smiled at me in understanding.

I listened to the judge talk, not really listening to his words but hearing his voice of authority. Suddenly, I was terrified. What if the jury did not believe me? What if my father went back to prison? My whole body was trembling and Agent Stements leaned down towards me. "Just breathe," he said softly. I closed my eyes and ignored everything around me, focusing on breathing slowly.

When my name was finally called to testify, Agent Stements stood and took my hand in his. He walked me all the way to the stand. "You've got this," he whispered before he walked away. I repeated the oath and sat down on the hard bench. Then I turned and looked at my father. He smiled at me, and some of the tension left my body.

Mr. Goldman walked towards me. He asked questions about how I grew up and I explained about my life in Kansas. He asked me what brought me to Colorado. I told about the two men in the café that had tried to abduct me and how I escaped with David who had brought me here to help me find answers.

"Did you ever see those two men again after that day?" he asked me. "Yes, they took me from my motel room at gunpoint and took me to my uncle, Jimmy Smaldone's house," I replied. "What memories do you have about your Uncle Jimmy?" he asked me. "Objection. Relevance to this case," the other attorney said.

"Your Honor, there is definitely relevance in this question," Mr. Goldman said. "I'll allow it," the judge replied. "The first time I met him, my mother and I were forced into a car where Jimmy and my grandfather waited for us. Jimmy pulled a gun on us. I was terrified, and I remember clinging to my mother tightly," I answered him.

"Do you have any other memories of you uncle?" he asked. I nodded and told about seeing him at the carnival the night my mother was killed and how he was watching me. Then I explained after he kidnapped me how I accused him of killing my mother and he admitted it. "He told me that Victor was weak. Victor couldn't bring himself to kill my mother, so Jimmy took it upon himself to do it. Victor had said she was dead to him, and

Jimmy took that to mean literally," I said, looking down at my hands in my lap.

"Was your father there at the carnival that night?" he asked me. "No, he got a phone call before we left and didn't come with us. He told me that he would come when he was done. When the men killed my mother and I ran through the woods, I fell down a steep incline. That was where my father found me," I explained.

"He had been driving to meet us, but he saw me tumbling down the incline on the side of the road. When he picked me up, I told him that my mother was dead. He put me in the car and turned the car around right there on the road. We drove through the night to Kansas where he left me with friends," I continued.

Mr. Goldman held up a large piece of paper that had already been submitted into evidence. From where I sat, I could see that it was a map. He walked over to the jury and showed them where the carnival had been set up, where the woods were that I had run through, and where the cliff I had fallen down was located. Then he pointed out the point in the road where I had landed and where my father had picked me up.

"Members of the jury, my client found his daughter after his wife had been killed. He turned the car around right here on this road. If he would have continued on to the carnival, it would have taken him an additional fifteen minutes to get there as the road curves around this way," he said, pointing at the map.

"If he had killed his wife and then somehow managed to find his daughter, and then got in his car and headed towards this road, the police would have passed his car. However, witnesses at the time claim to have seen his car on this road just five minutes after the shooting. Five minutes was all it took for five-year-old Aurora to run from here to here," he said, again pointing at the map.

After a few questions from the other attorney, I was told I could take my seat. I sat down next to Agent Stements and waited for what would happen next. To my surprise, Elizabeth was the next witness called to the stand. The bailiff opened the door of the courtroom, and I watched as Elizabeth made her way to the front.

She had my full attention as she explained to the jury everything that she had told David and me when we visited her. She explained about being an escort for

Jimmy and how he had promised to get her away from that life if she agreed to testify against my father. I felt the tears rolling down my face as she turned and looked at me.

"I owe you a sincere apology," she told me from the stand. "Because of me, you lost nineteen years with your father, and I can never give that back to you. But I want to thank you for giving me this opportunity to make things right," she said, and I nodded at her.

The leather-bound book was also entered as evidence. Mr. Goldman explained that the thick book had been Victor Smaldone's and Jimmy had inherited it. It held a notation from the night of my mother's death. Only initials were listed, but two sets of initials were paid ten thousand dollars each. He explained that Abigail's name was written beside it and her name had a line drawn through it.

Mr. Goldman looked up at the judge. "No further questions. The defense rests it's case," he said. After a few words from the judge, he sent the jury to deliberate and court was done. "What now?" I turned and asked Agent Stements. "Now we go back to the hotel and wait for the jury to decide," he said gently. I sighed heavily and watched as an officer led my father away.

When we stepped back into the hallway, I saw David immediately. He stepped towards me. "How did it go?" he asked me. "I'm not sure. I have never been in court before," I told him honestly. "I think it looks good," Agent Stements told him and I looked up at him in surprise. What he said next surprised me even more.

"I think Aurora could use your presence right now. Would you like to take a ride with us?" he asked David. David looked at me with a tender smile on his face. "Absolutely," he said softly, his eye never leaving mine. With my hand in his, the two agents led us out into the crowd of reporters. I was not tense this time, and I felt David squeeze my hand a little tighter as we made our way to the car and got inside.

Chapter 22

Back at the hotel, David took my hand again. He did not let go, even after we sat down on the couch in the living room. David spoke with the agents and I leaned my head against his shoulder. David looked down at me and then put his arm around me, pulling me closer against him. My head rested against his chest.

The next thing I heard was David calling my name. I opened my eyes and looked up at him smiling down at me. "How long was I asleep?" I asked him. "About three and a half hours," he told me. It really did not surprise me. I had not had a decent night of sleep since coming here.

Agent Stements walked towards me with a plate in his hands. He handed it to me. "You missed lunch," he said kindly. "As soon as you finish that, we have to head back to the courthouse. The jury is ready with their verdict," he told me. I took the plate he held out to me and ate quickly. David handed me a bottle of water and I took a drink then stood from the couch. "I'm ready," I told the men in the room. David took my hand once again and we made our way back out to the car.

At the courthouse, we again fought our way through the reporters and into the building. David gave me a hug before I walked into the courtroom with the two agents. We sat down and waited for the jury and the judge. I watched my father being led into the room and he took a seat next to Mr. Goldman once more. He gave me a tender smile before turning to face the front of the room.

I could not help grabbing a hand of each of the agents beside me when the judge asked the foreperson if the jury had reached a unanimous decision. "We have, Your Honor," the woman replied. "You may read the verdict aloud," the judge said. I closed my eyes and waited for the woman to speak.

"On the three counts of murder in the first degree, we, the jury, find the defendant not guilty," I heard him say. Suddenly, it seemed my ears were full of noise, like the sound of thunder. My breath caught in my throat, and my body was frozen on the bench. It was not until my father stood from his chair and turned and looked at me that air rushed back into my lungs.

I stood from the bench and hurried towards my father. People were moving past me to exit the courtroom, but I kept my eyes on my father. When I reached him, I stopped in front of him and my eyes met his. He had tears in his eyes, and I realized that I did too.

When he opened his arms to me, I stepped forward and wrapped my arms around him, feeling and hearing the sobs from both of us. We stood like that for quite some time before I felt a hand on my shoulder. I turned and looked up at David who had approached from behind me.

"Mr. Davis, congratulations," he said, reaching out his hand to my father. Instead of shaking his hand, my father grabbed his hand and pulled him against us, hugging him tightly as well. I laughed and reached my arm around David. I had never felt this happy.

A few minutes later, we all stepped back from each other. My father and I still studied each other. Nineteen years had changed both of us. David had told me that he had shown my father pictures of me when he went to visit him when we had first arrived in Colorado. "I can't believe you did it," he said, looking from me to David with a wide smile on his face.

"What happens now?" I asked, and Agent Stements stepped forward. He had been standing a few feet behind David, and I had not noticed him until he spoke. "Now, the three of you will go into protective custody until you testify against Jimmy Smaldone," he answered. I knew that Jimmy had contacts everywhere and none of us would be safe until he was put away.

I took one of David's hands in mine and with my other hand I reached for my father's hand. Then I looked up at Agent Stements. "Together?" I asked him seriously. I watched the smile spread across his face. "I don't think you would have it any other way," he told me.

EPILOGUE

Five days later, David drove up to a ranch style house in College Grove, Tennessee. My father was in the passenger seat and I sat in the backseat. When the car stopped in front of the garage, David popped the trunk. We all got out of the car and we each took our suitcases from the trunk. Together we walked towards the porch.

It was a brick home, not too big but not too small. We already knew that it had three bedrooms and two bathrooms. There was a nice sized porch on the front, and I noticed the three chairs and a small round table there. They had set up the house for the three of us. The house also had a two-car garage that was attached.

David found the key on his ring and unlocked the front door. We stepped into a comfortable looking living room that had plenty of room for the sofa and love seat as well as two end tables and a coffee table. It was open to the kitchen and separated by a bar with three bar stools. There was an alcove in the kitchen that had a square table with four chairs around it.

After exploring these rooms, we walked into the small hallway on the far-left wall of the living room from where we had entered the house. There were two doors and the first revealed a large sized laundry room. The next door we discovered was the master bedroom. David and I had already agreed it would be my father's room. He set his bag inside the room and we moved to the hallway on the other side of the living room.

There were two bedrooms and a bathroom, and another door revealed a linen closet. I chose the smaller bedroom. Both rooms had double beds, but I did not need a lot of space. All I had were my clothes. David had his laptop and a book to write, and the other bedroom had a desk. It would be perfect for him.

The next few months in hiding would be the perfect time for David to write our story. He would be living with the main two characters of his book. He had already sent articles about the case, and how my father had been proven innocent, to be published in the paper he wrote for and the several magazines as well. His article about the resort that was going to be built included the information that the new owner of the property had been arrested for running a prostitution ring, racketeering, embezzlement, several counts of murder, and kidnapping. There would be no resort coming to that small town.

After my father's retrial, Victor Smaldone had a stroke and now he would be spending the last of his days in a nursing home. He was bed-ridden, and the doctors did not think he would be around much longer. Marybeth had indeed known about her husband's prostitution ring and she was arrested as an accomplice. David had been the first to report on all these details.

After we all got settled into our rooms, the next step was grocery shopping. David and I in our new identities were husband and wife. I was Andrea Jones and David was Anthony Jones. My father would still be my father, but he was now Thomas Zander. We had practiced for the last few days only calling each other by these names.

A little while later, David and I went to the grocery store. We had been given money for groceries, and that evening I cooked dinner for the three of us. It had been a long time since either my father or I had laughed, but we laughed a lot over dinner. After dinner, my father decided to go to his room and rest with a book. David and I cleaned up the kitchen together.

When the last dish was put away, David took my hand and led me to the couch in the living room. I sat down next to him, but he did not release my hand. "Aurora," he said, turning and picking up my other hand in his. I started to remind him to use my fake name, but he reached his finger to my lips to stop me from speaking.

"What I want to say, I can only say to Aurora," he told me tenderly. I waited patiently for him to continue. "I don't want to go any further with this until I tell you that I love you. I know it hasn't been long since we officially met, but I know what I feel. I know that I love you," he said softly.

I did not even hesitate to reply. "David, I love you too," I told him. Finally, I watched in anticipation as he leaned towards me and our lips met. I felt his hand on the back of my neck and my arms reached around him. Nothing in my life had ever felt as right as this moment with David.